SIGNS
and
WONDERS

Also by Philip Gulley
in Large Print:

Home to Harmony
Just Shy of Harmony

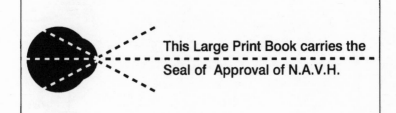

SIGNS
and
WONDERS

Philip Gulley

Thorndike Press • Waterville, Maine

Published in 2003 by arrangement with HarperSanFranciso, a division of HarperCollins Publishers, Inc.

Thorndike Press® Large Print Americana.

The tree indicium is a trademark of Thorndike Press.

The text of this Large Print edition is unabridged.
Other aspects of the book may vary from the original edition.

Set in 16 pt. Plantin by Christina S. Huff.

Printed in the United States on permanent paper.

Library of Congress Cataloging-in-Publication Data

Gulley, Philip.
    Signs and wonders : a harmony novel / Philip Gulley.
        p. cm.
    ISBN 0-7862-5639-7 (lg. print : hc : alk. paper)
    1. Harmony (Ind. : Imaginary place) — Fiction.   2. City and town life — Fiction.   3. Indiana — Fiction.
    4. Quakers — Fiction.   5. Clergy — Fiction.   6. Large type books.   I. Title.
PS3557.U449S56 2003b
813'.54—dc21   2003052682

To Joan and the boys and
the people of Fairfield Friends Meeting

National Association for Visually Handicapped
serving the partially seeing

As the Founder/CEO of NAVH, the only national health agency solely devoted to those who, although not totally blind, have an eye disease which could lead to serious visual impairment, I am pleased to recognize Thorndike Press* as one of the leading publishers in the large print field.

Founded in 1954 in San Francisco to prepare large print textbooks for partially seeing children, NAVH became the pioneer and standard setting agency in the preparation of large type.

Today, those publishers who meet our standards carry the prestigious "Seal of Approval" indicating high quality large print. We are delighted that Thorndike Press is one of the publishers whose titles meet these standards. We are also pleased to recognize the significant contribution Thorndike Press is making in this important and growing field.

Lorraine H. Marchi, L.H.D.
Founder/CEO
NAVH

* Thorndike Press encompasses the following imprints: Thorndike, Wheeler, Walker and Large Print Press.

Contents

One

The Tenderloin Queen

The summer Barbara Gardner turned sixteen, she was crowned the Tenderloin Queen by the Lawrence County Pork Producers. She received a fifty-dollar scholarship, twenty pounds of sausage, and a one-year subscription to the *Hoosier Farmer* magazine. Plus, she had her picture taken as the pork producers president placed the Tenderloin Queen crown on her head. The picture ran in the September 1977 edition of the *Hoosier Farmer* magazine, which she's saved in her hope chest.

Her reign as Miss Tenderloin led to a fascination with contests, and since then she'd entered every one she could. She'd won two free windows, a year's supply of Grape-Nuts cereal, and carpet cleaning for three rooms. But she hadn't won anything lately and believed she was overdue for a victory. So when she was shopping at the Kroger back in March and saw the disc jockey from

WEAK selling raffle tickets for a Caribbean trip, she bought ten chances at a dollar each.

Ordinarily, Barbara never paid money to enter a contest, but it was for a good cause. They were raising money to help Wayne and Sally Fleming pay the hospital bills for Sally's leukemia. It was just one of the many fund-raisers held for Sally. A lot of people worked a goodly number of hours to raise money, only to have Sally healed by the Reverend Johnny LaCosta over the television airwaves. A few people complained that maybe the Reverend could have been more considerate and healed her before they'd gone to all the trouble of having the fund-raisers.

When Barbara filled out the raffle tickets, she had a premonition she'd win. She was so confident she went to Kivett's Five and Dime and bought a new bathing suit she'd seen on the mannequin in the front window the day before. Ned Kivett had ordered the mannequin all the way from New Jersey. His old mannequin had worn out after thirty years. Kids drew mustaches on her, and she'd been kidnapped twice at Halloween. Ned wasn't all that keen about letting her go, but her arm had fallen off, and her hair was so sparse it looked like rows of corn.

The new mannequin came in early

March. She arrived in a long box delivered by the UPS man on a Monday afternoon. She didn't look anything like the old mannequin. She looked real. When Ned opened the box, he saw her lying there naked on a bed of Styrofoam peanuts and turned away, embarrassed. "Excuse me, ma'am," he said quickly. He averted his gaze as he helped her from the box, then draped her with a bedsheet until his wife could dress her in a bathing suit. The sheet only made things worse, emphasizing the very features he wished to conceal. He kept her in the back room for a week before working up the nerve to bring her out in public. It was awkward carrying her — he wasn't sure where to put his hands. So he put her in a cart instead and wheeled her through the store to the front window, where he set her in a lawn chair.

That's where Barbara saw her as she was walking past on her way home from the Kroger. She stopped and looked. It reminded her of herself, back when she was the Tenderloin Queen. She bought the bathing suit, took it home, tried it on, and looked at herself in the mirror. If she stood sideways, she could barely make out the faint web of varicose veins. At least her thighs didn't touch, which wasn't bad for a

11

woman with two kids. Not bad, she thought. Not bad at all.

Barbara's been exercising. Every afternoon she walks with Mabel Morrison a mile out into the country, then back home. It was Mabel's idea. She had turned seventy-five back in February, and Doctor Neely had told her she needed to exercise, so she'd asked Barbara to walk with her. It's been good for Barbara, too. Being the pastor's wife, she can't talk with just anyone for fear what she said would get around, and Mabel isn't prone to gossip.

Mabel used to be Catholic, but got mad that they didn't allow women priests, so she quit going. But she's good at keeping secrets, so Barbara tells her a lot of things, mostly about her marriage with Sam.

"He never talks. He comes home and flops down in his chair, then eats supper, and then is back out the door to go to some church meeting. I'm getting kinda tired of it."

"That's how my Harold was. He was either at the store or sleeping. We never even went on a vacation. Twenty-one years straight we went to St. Louis for the International Shoe Company's customer appreciation dinner. That was it. Some years, we wouldn't even stay the night. He'd make us drive back that night so we could be at the store the next day."

They talk about other things, too. They discuss theology. Mabel's been reading books written by a liberal Episcopalian, and she thinks he might be onto something. He believes the Apostle Paul probably never said for women to keep silent in church, that some male chauvinist probably snuck that in later. Mabel's been writing to the Unitarians and is thinking of starting a Unitarian church in Harmony. "Somewhere where you can think things about God without someone telling you you're wrong," she told Barbara.

They discuss politics. On the last Election Day, Mabel went to the meetinghouse to vote, and when she asked for a write-in ballot, Dale Hinshaw wouldn't give her one. "Don't rock the boat," he told her. "Just vote for the Republican. That's what Harold would have wanted you to do."

There was a time when Mabel would have given in, but not anymore. She's seventy-five years old and wants to do a little boat rocking. She leaned down, close to Dale's face, and said in a low voice, "You give me a write-in ballot or I'll have you arrested."

Barbara believes in equality, but she worries Mabel might have gone off the deep end. Still, she's interesting to be around. She's never known anyone quite like Mabel, someone who speaks her mind so freely. She's used to smiling when people annoy her. It's the minister's wife in her. Don't say what you think, don't do what you want, just smile and be pleasant, no matter what.

She has a college degree in education and taught for four years while Sam was in seminary, so they put her on the Christian Education Committee, but pay her no mind. Barbara suggested at the March meeting that they no longer use the *Sword of the Lord* curriculum, because it upset the children. Fern Hampton pointed out that they'd been using the *Sword of the Lord* curriculum for over twenty years and said that the problem with today's youth was that they heard too much about God's love and not enough about the sword of the Lord. Then she said Barbara might want to reflect on whether she truly loved the Lord.

Barbara didn't say anything; she just smiled. But ever since then she's been wanting to go away for a while with Sam. Just the two of them going someplace where there aren't any church people. So in early April when WEAK Radio called to say her name had been drawn for the Caribbean Trip Giveaway, she was so excited she hung up the phone and had to call back to get the details. A trip for two to the Caribbean for seven days. All expenses paid, plus five hundred dollars spending money.

The Caribbean! When Barbara was in eighth grade, she'd gone on a school trip to Washington, D.C. She'd ridden all night on a bus, eleven hours straight. That was the longest trip she'd ever taken. She'd never even been on an airplane. Now she was going to the Caribbean.

She'd seen a travelogue on the Caribbean at the library back in February. It had been a cold, dreary week, so Miss Rudy, the librarian, ran a notice in the *Harmony Herald* that she would be showing a Caribbean travelogue that Friday. Sam and Barbara took their boys and went. They sat in folding chairs while Miss Rudy ran the projector, aiming the picture at the wall over the drinking fountain.

The travelogue was mostly slides from when Harvey and Eunice Muldock went to Puerto Rico in 1971 to attend a Plymouth dealership convention. Harvey had taken the pictures, lots of palm trees and sunsets and beaches with an occasional picture of Eunice in her bathing suit. To everyone's great relief, Miss Rudy didn't let those pictures linger too long on the drinking-fountain wall.

The travelogue had whet Barbara's appetite for the exotic. Now to win the trip, to actually be headed to the Caribbean, was almost more than she could bear. She called her parents to tell them, then walked down to the meetinghouse to tell Sam. She'd thought about calling him, then decided she wanted to see the look on his face.

His head was buried in a book. She knocked on the door frame. He looked up. "Hey."

"Hey, yourself."

"What brings you down here?"

"Oh, nothing much. Guess who just called me?"

"I give up. Who?"

"A man from the radio station."

"Oh yeah."

"Yeah."

"What'd he have to say?"

"Nothing much. He just wanted to tell me that I'd won a trip for two to the Caribbean. Just you and me, Sam. My folks are gonna come up and watch the kids. We leave next week." She began to laugh.

Sam looked at the calendar on his desk, then frowned. "Gee, honey. I'm busy next week. Remember, it's the annual planning meeting for the Christian Education Committee. I told Fern I'd be there."

Barbara groaned. "You've got to be kidding."

"No, I'm not. I made a promise, and so did you. You're on the committee, too."

"Oh, Sam, they'll understand. Just call and tell them we won't be there. They'll understand."

Sam leaned back in his chair and thought for a moment. "Nope, I don't think so. I've given my word. That's all a man really has, his word."

Barbara didn't talk to him for two days, except to ask if he could pass the salt. "But you don't have to do it if it interferes with your job. I wouldn't want you to pass the salt if it distracts you from your work. After all, it's more important than anything else."

He knew better than to say anything back.

Then one morning, later in the week, while she and Mabel were walking, she invited Mabel to go with her, and Mabel jumped at the chance. Mabel had never been anywhere except to the International Shoe Company's annual customer appreciation dinner in St. Louis. She was ready to hit the road. "Of course, if your husband changes his mind, you take him and I'll understand."

Barbara kept hoping Sam would change

his mind, but he didn't. She'd even tried on her new bathing suit in front of him the night before she left. "Nice," he'd said. Then he said, "Say, do you have any ideas about Sunday school you want me to pass on to the committee?"

She left the next morning. She didn't bother to wake Sam, just showered and dressed and stood outside on the porch with her suitcase waiting for Mabel to come past in her Buick. They drove to the airport, two women who'd always come in second to their husbands' jobs. They parked in the long-term lot and took a bus to the terminal. It was a quick flight — an hour and twenty minutes to Miami, then a smaller plane to St. Thomas. Neither one had ever been on an airplane. They prayed the entire way, their seat belts cinched tightly across their laps.

They picked up their suitcases from the luggage carousel, then walked outside to get a taxi to the hotel. It wasn't much like the hotel in the brochure. There was one double bed in their room. The bedspread had a cigarette burn. The bathroom faucet dripped, and the sink had a rust stain. It wasn't exactly on the beach either, like the radio station had promised. But if you stood on the balcony you could smell the ocean.

All of those things didn't bother Barbara

nearly as much as Sam not coming with her.

It took two days for it to dawn on Sam that he should have gone with her to the Caribbean. It was Tuesday night. He was lying in bed, thinking of her, wondering what she was doing that very moment. The brochures from the radio station were lying on the nightstand. Sam thumbed through them. They showed pictures of tanned young men playing volleyball. Sam grew slightly alarmed. The 1977 Tenderloin Queen, with her husband a thousand miles away, would be fair game.

The annual planning meeting for the Christian Education Committee was the next evening, but it no longer seemed all that crucial. He woke up early, called the radio station to find out where Barbara was staying, dropped his sons off at his parents' house, and drove to the airport. He called Fern Hampton from a pay phone inside the terminal to tell her he wouldn't be at the meeting. "You'll have to carry on without me."

"I forgot you were even going to be there," Fern said. It didn't exactly buoy his spirits to learn that the very committee costing him his marriage wasn't even aware of his sacrifice.

It took most of the day and most of his

credit-card limit to reach St. Thomas. He had to fly through Pittsburgh and Atlanta, then to Miami, where he caught the last plane to St. Thomas. It was midnight before he reached the hotel where Barbara and Mabel were staying. He knocked on the door, but they weren't in their room. He was too late. He thought of the tanned young men in the brochure. Twelve years of marriage down the drain. He could hardly blame her. His indifference had driven her into the arms of another.

Across the street at the casino, Barbara and Mabel were playing the slot machines. It had been Barbara's idea, something she'd always wanted to do. Being the wife of a Quaker pastor didn't permit certain indulgences, one of which was playing the slot machines. But in St. Thomas they didn't know she was a minister's wife.

In St. Thomas she didn't have to be a role model. She could be a regular person. She could go into a casino and, if by chance she grew thirsty, sip a certain cold beverage not usually associated with ministers' wives. And if a tanned young man sat at the slot machine next to her and smiled, what would be the harm in smiling back? And if he had been the one to buy her that cold beverage, well, it would have been rude not to accept, wouldn't it? Still, she was a minister's wife and to gamble and smile at a tanned young man made her feel a little guilty.

Barbara and Mabel spent the last of their quarters, waved good-bye to the tanned young man, and crossed the street to their hotel. Sam was sitting on the steps outside their door, his head in his hands.

He looked up as Barbara and Mabel came up the stairs.

"Sam, is that you? What are you doing here? Is everything all right? Are the boys okay?"

"Everything's fine, honey. I just missed you, that's all."

He took a step toward her. "I'm sorry I didn't come with you. It was thoughtless of me."

"It certainly was," Mabel said.

"Mabel, why don't you go on up to the room," Barbara said. "I think I'll be okay alone with him."

Mabel walked past Barbara and frowned at Sam.

"I'm sorry," Sam said again. "Please forgive me. I know I was wrong. That's why I came here. I've been waiting outside your door all this time. I was worried something had happened to you. Are you okay? Where were you?" He was almost afraid to hear the answer.

Barbara hung her head. "I'd rather not say."

Sam didn't press her for an answer. If she and Mabel had enjoyed the company of tanned young men, he had only himself to blame. He felt nauseous at the thought of his wife gazing dreamily at a tanned young man. But if she could forgive his thoughtlessness, he could surely forgive her. That's what marriage was about, after all — forgiveness and consideration and not badgering your spouse for an answer you might not like.

"Please forgive me," he said.

She took a step toward him. "It hurt that you didn't come with me. It made me a little crazy. I've done things tonight I'm not exactly proud of."

Sam held up his hand. "Don't say another word. I take full responsibility. I should never have let you come here without me."

She hugged him. "I love you."

"I love you, honey." He hugged her back.

They suddenly felt the urge to be alone.

They went into the hotel room. Mabel was lying in the double bed. "I've called room service for a cot," she said. "I'm sure it'll be fine for you, Sam."

"Mabel, Barbara and I thought you might

enjoy having your own room. We'd be happy to pay for it."

"Oh, no. You kids save your money. I don't mind sharing a room with you."

They stayed four more days. Sam took pictures of palm trees and sunsets and beaches with an occasional picture of Barbara in her new bathing suit. They had slides made, which they gave to Miss Rudy, who showed them the following Friday night on the wall over the drinking fountain.

Sam and Barbara took the boys and went. There was a good crowd. The high-school basketball season had ended and there wasn't much on television. They had to set up extra chairs. A lot of the church members were there. They were a little shocked to see the minister's wife in a bathing suit. There were a few raised eyebrows. Miss Rudy blushed. Barbara thought, Not bad for a woman with two kids.

Sam squeezed her hand and whispered in her ear, "Who's that lovely young lady?"

"I believe it's the 1977 Lawrence County Tenderloin Queen," she whispered back.

Every now and then, a picture of a tanned young man flashed up on the wall. Just often enough to make Sam appreciate what he had and might have lost.

Two
Spring in Harmony

The surest harbinger of spring is the opening of the Dairy Queen. It's the signal to bring up the porch furniture from the basement, push the snowblower back to the corner of the garage, and sharpen the blades on the lawn mower. Windows are propped open, curtains are washed, and dead flies are vacuumed from the window sills.

The Dairy Queen used to open on Ash Wednesday, until Father McLaughlin at the Catholic church got up a petition in which Oscar and Livinia Purdy, the owners of the Dairy Queen, were cautioned to honor the Lord or else. Oscar and Livinia didn't fight it. They stayed a little longer at the Sunny Daze Trailer Park outside Pensacola, Florida, and opened the Dairy Queen the first Monday in May instead. When people complained about the late opening, Oscar said, "Tell it to the Catholics."

In early May, Oscar hauls his ladder from

home and changes the sign from *CLOSED FOR THE SEASON* to *OPENING THIS MONDAY — FREE SPRINKLES ON EVERY CONE*. Livinia cleans the ice-cream machines and washes the windows. Bob Miles from the *Harmony Herald* stops past and snaps a picture of the preparations.

The Dairy Queen was built in 1967 on the corner of Main and Washington, where the train station stood before Oscar and Livinia bought it from the Great Northern Railway Company and hired Bud Matthews to knock it down with his bulldozer. Although it was their building to do with as they pleased, it seemed an unspeakable violation. There was talk of boycotting the Dairy Queen, and things didn't calm down until Oscar offered free sprinkles on every cone. They're good sprinkles — peanutty crunchies with red and blue sprinkles mixed in.

When Bud knocked down the station they found a time capsule, welded shut, with *1857* etched on the top. Bud carried it down to the *Herald* building and stored it in the back corner. The plan was to save the capsule in case the president ever visited and open it then to commemorate the event. Richard Nixon's third cousin, Lucy Milhous, lived just outside of town, which everyone hoped would lure him to town.

Every December he'd send her a Christmas card, which she displayed in the front window of the Rexall. She'd invite him to the family reunion, but with a war on, he couldn't come. He hoped she understood. Then when the war ended, he got in trouble and didn't go out much after that.

The years passed, and the time capsule was forgotten. Then Bob Miles came across it when he was cleaning out his office. He had been intending to clean the *Herald* office for a number of years, but the pressures of a weekly deadline hadn't allowed it. So the first week of May, he wrote, *There will be no edition of the* Herald *next week due to office renovations.* He thought "office renovations" sounded better than "hauling a bunch of stuff to the town dump," which was what he had in mind to do.

The *Herald* was begun in the 1850s by Bob's great-grandfather, the original Robert J. Miles. It was his idea to store items of historical interest in the back corner of his office in the event Harmony ever built a museum. When the trains stopped running, there was talk of turning the station into a museum, but then the Purdys knocked it down to build the Dairy Queen and that ended the discussion. Meanwhile, Bob was stuck with all that old junk cluttering up his office.

There was a lightbulb purported to be the first lightbulb in Harmony. There was the telephone headset from when Hazel Rutledge was the telephone operator and had the switchboard in her kitchen pantry. There was a sword from the Civil War, which Bob's grandfather had bent while prying open a can of paint. There was a brick from the Harmony Institute for Virtuous Young Ladies, which closed in 1921 due to a shortage of virtuous young ladies. On a top shelf, in a dusty wooden crate, were three bones with a note that read: *Found on the Albert Deming farm on May 5, 1932. Might be cow bones, or possibly dinosaur bones.*

The time capsule was in back of the box of bones. By standing on his tiptoes, Bob could just reach it. He slid it across the shelf and lifted it down. It was thick with dust. He wiped it down with a rag and that was when he noticed the numbers *1857* etched in the top. He picked up the time capsule and shook it. There was a rattling sound. It sounded like money. Maybe there're some old coins in there, Bob thought.

The week before, he'd read in a magazine of a man who'd found a coin in his pocket change worth a thousand dollars. He crossed his office and locked the front door, then took the sword and tried to pry the capsule open. The sword snapped in half. He wrapped it in old newspapers and hid it in the bottom of the trash can.

He carried the time capsule to his car, drove home, and set it on the workbench in his garage. The capsule was welded shut. He took his hacksaw down from its peg and began to saw, but the steel was thick and it was slow going. He thought about asking Harvey Muldock if he could borrow his cutting torch, but decided against it. Harvey would want half of whatever was in the time capsule, and Bob wasn't of a mind to share.

He wasn't sure what was in there, but he hoped it was worth a lot of money. He wanted out of the newspaper business. He was tired of the grind. He wanted to shut the *Herald* down and do a little traveling, but first he needed money. He'd never saved any money. He'd always counted on hitting it big, maybe buying a painting at a garage sale for ten dollars and then finding out it was worth three million.

On Saturday nights, he and Arvella watched *Antiques Roadshow* on television. People would drag in junk worth thousands of dollars. It was stuff Bob saw as a kid — Coca-Cola signs and tables and ugly glass vases. He told Arvella, "One of these days

28

I'm gonna clean out our attic and go on that show. I bet we got a million dollars worth of stuff up there."

He didn't mention to Arvella about finding the time capsule. He'd hidden it behind the lawn mower in the corner of the garage, and after Arvella went to bed, he'd go out and work on it with his hacksaw. After three nights of sawing, the last of the metal gave way, and the lid clattered to the garage floor. Bob peered inside.

For a good-sized box, there wasn't much in there — an 1857 almanac and a Queen Victoria Bible, printed in 1851. It was the King James Bible with all the racy verses edited out. The Song of Solomon had been removed entirely, and David and Bathsheba had confined their affections to a brief handshake.

At the bottom of the box was a coin. It had a shapely woman on one side and an eagle on the other. Underneath the woman was the number *1804.*

Bob read the date twice. 1804! He let out a low whistle. Nearly two hundred years old. Now that's gotta be worth something, he thought. He put the coin in his pocket.

There was an old newspaper in the box, the very first edition of the *Herald.* It didn't look much different from the paper the week before. The weather forecast was in the top left corner: *Mostly sunny, unless it rains. Seasonal temperatures expected, though variations might occur.* The church news was on the third page, and the "Ten Years Ago Today" column was on the second.

The next morning, Bob drove to the city to a coin shop near downtown, just off the Interstate. The sign was hanging loose on one bolt, and there were bars on the windows. The door was locked. Bob tapped on the glass. A man in a T-shirt peered out at Bob, then unbolted the door and let him in.

"Whatcha want?"

Bob showed him the coin. The man thumbed through a book, wetting his finger as he turned the pages.

"Let's see. That's an 1804 silver dollar. These old silver dollars aren't worth as much as people think. Coin market's slow these days. I can give you eight hundred for it."

Eight hundred dollars! Bob tried not to appear overly excited.

"Well, I don't know. I was thinking it'd maybe be worth a little more than that. I was thinking it was worth at least a thousand dollars, a coin like that. Maybe I oughta take it somewhere else."

"Nine hundred then, and you're getting a real bargain there, mister."

Nine hundred dollars! Bob was beside himself. This was better than *Antiques Roadshow.*

Bob tried to look pained. These sharpies from the city weren't the only ones who knew how to drive a bargain. Thirty years of buying cars from Harvey Muldock had honed Bob's skill.

Bob reached across the counter and took the coin. "Nah, I think I'll just hold on to it. Maybe my grandkids will want it one day."

He didn't even have any grandchildren; he just said that.

Bob put the coin in his pocket. "Thanks just the same. Sorry to take up your time."

He turned toward the door.

"Okay, then. A thousand even."

He paid Bob with ten one-hundred-dollar bills from a safe in the back room.

"What about a receipt?" Bob said.

"Well, sure, I mean if you want to pay taxes on that money, that's okay by me."

"Well, maybe I don't need a receipt after all. Why bother the government with all that paperwork."

Bob didn't see any need to tell Arvella what he'd done. She'd been after him for a new refrigerator, but he didn't see the point of it. The old one was running fine.

"A little paint and it'll look like new," he'd told her. "Those old Kelvinators are good for thirty or forty years anyway."

No, there was no reason to tell her.

He was feeling prosperous. He stopped at the Dairy Queen, bought an ice-cream cone with sprinkles, gave Livinia a dollar, and told her to keep the change.

He hid the money in his garage, in the grass catcher of his lawn mower. Arvella would never find it there. He lay awake that night thinking of closing down the *Herald* and maybe going into the coin business. A man with his bargaining skills could do well for himself. The next week he drove to the bank in Cartersburg and bought a certificate of deposit at 4.25 percent interest. He told them to send the paperwork to his office, not his house.

He wasn't sure what to do with the Queen Victoria Bible. He wanted to show it to someone, but didn't for fear they'd ask him where he got it. He put it at the bottom of a box of paperback mysteries he dropped off at the library for the annual book sale while Miss Rudy, the librarian, was gone to lunch. He didn't need her asking a bunch of questions. As old as she was, she was probably there when they put the Bible in the time capsule.

He stopped past the Coffee Cup for a bite to eat. Heather Darnell was waiting tables. Heather had sort of graduated from high school the year before and had already been fired from a number of jobs. Ned Kivett had hired her as a checkout girl, but had to let her go when she kept giving back too much change. Then she worked at the nursing home, but got to watching the soap operas and forgot to clean people. When the place got to smelling, they had to let her go.

Vinny and Penny Toricelli had hired her as a favor to her parents. It was working out well, so long as the diners weren't picky about getting what they'd ordered. Although Heather wasn't big on details, she was very pretty and the old men at the Coffee Cup were reluctant to complain.

Heather Darnell in her waitress uniform is a walking testimony to the beauty of God's creation. She touches their arms while they order and after she's done that, they don't seem to mind that she brought lima beans instead of corn or filled their tea glass with diet soda.

"Oh, no, this is fine. I like a diet drink every now and then. I've been meaning to lose a few pounds anyway."

Heather laughs and tells them they don't need to lose weight, that they look pretty good to her. They suck in their bellies and sit up a little straighter.

Heather hands them a menu, which they pretend to read while she touches their arm. They take their time, like they've never seen that menu, even though Vinny hasn't changed it in twenty years. Then, because she'll get the order wrong anyway, they tell her to bring whatever looks good.

She brought Bob meat loaf. While he was eating, the siren down at the fire station sounded the noon whistle. Vinny flipped on the TV behind the counter to watch the news from the city. They gave the weather and told who won the ball game, then reported on a burglary and a police chase. That made everyone feel good. It delights them to hear of troubles in other places, as if it confirms their wisdom for living where they do.

"Geez, would you look at that," Vinny said. "It's nuts up there. Who'd want to live there? Not me, that's for sure."

There was a commercial break, and then the news came back on.

"There's good news for one man in our city today," the TV announcer said. "Yesterday, Herbert Green, the owner of a local coin shop, sold a rare 1804 draped-bust American silver dollar at Sotheby's Auction in New York City for four million dollars! Mr. Green is closing his coin shop and planning on doing some traveling."

Vinny let out a low whistle. "Geeminey Christmas, would you look at that. That guy's set for life. Four million bucks for a silver dollar. Man, oh man. Wouldn't you like to have that kind of luck?"

Bob stood up from the booth, went to the cash register, and paid his bill. He didn't leave a tip. He wasn't feeling all that prosperous anymore. He walked to the *Herald* office and sat at his desk, thinking. There's a lesson in here somewhere, he told himself. I'm not sure what it is, but if I think long enough, I suspect it'll come to me.

Meanwhile, he had a paper to get out. He opened his desk, pulled out the picture of Oscar Purdy standing on his ladder changing the Dairy Queen sign, pasted it on the first page, and wrote underneath it: *Oscar and Livinia Purdy ready themselves for another year of ice cream! As always, there will be free sprinkles on every cone!*

He tried hard not to think how many ice-cream cones he could have bought with four million dollars.

People feel kind of sorry for Bob Miles. It's not easy being a journalist in a town where nothing happens. In the spring, the only things to write about are the opening of the Dairy Queen and the annual library book sale, which Miss Rudy holds the tail end of May.

The Harmony Public Library was built in 1903 with a grant from Andrew Carnegie. Up until then, the library had occupied the parlor of Ora Crandell, who was also the town's first librarian by virtue of owning more books than anyone else in town. When Ora Crandell died in 1902, she left the town her books, which are now displayed in the Ora Crandell Memorial Bookcase in the ladies' rest room. When they added indoor plumbing in 1913, the bookcase was too heavy to move, so they built the rest room around it.

Before her death, Ora Crandell had applied for a Carnegie grant, which was approved, and a new library was erected in 1903 east of the town square. Shortly after that, as rumor has it, Miss Rudy was employed as the librarian.

The Harmony Public Library, ostensibly a democratic organization, more closely resembles a South American dictatorship. The first week a book is overdue, Miss Rudy calls your home. The second week, she prints your name in the library column of the *Harmony Herald.* The third week, she sends Bernie, the policeman, to your house. If those measures fail, she places a lien on your home. There is no due process, no appeal to a higher court. There is no voting Miss Rudy out of office. She has the only key to the library. She keeps it on a chain around her neck, and no one's ever had the courage to retrieve it.

So it was that the meeting of the Library Board to plot the overthrow of Miss Rudy was held in secret in the basement of Owen Stout's home. The whole board was there, all three members, huddled around the laundry table, conspiring.

Lorraine Belcher suggested poisoning the postage stamps Miss Rudy kept in the top drawer of her desk. "We could maybe put a few drops of arsenic on the back of the stamps. The good thing about arsenic is that it kills a person real slow. They'll never be able to link it to us."

"My Lord, we don't want to hurt her," Judy Iverson said. "Why don't we just tell her it's time she retired and offer to name a room after her?"

"Won't work," said Owen Stout. "We tried that fifteen years ago. She barricaded herself in the library for three days. Wouldn't come out and wouldn't let anyone in. We had to shut off the water to get her out."

"We have to do something," Lorraine said. "We're the laughingstock of the library district. We don't have computers. We only made thirty-two dollars at our last book sale. And with people grouching about taxes, we need someone who can raise money. Someone younger, who isn't so bossy."

"We're gonna have to let her go, that's all there is to it," Owen said. "We need a volunteer. Who wants to tell her she's fired?"

"Why don't you tell her?" Lorraine asked. "You're the president of the board."

"Ordinarily, I would, but since I'm her lawyer it'd probably be a conflict of interest. She might want to hire me to sue the board for age discrimination. Why don't you tell her, Judy?"

"I don't think so. I have two children to think of. It's the quiet types that go crazy. I can't risk it."

"Well, I'm not gonna tell her. I had to tell her fifteen years ago," Lorraine said. "It's someone else's turn."

Owen sat at the laundry table, quiet and pensive, lawyer-like. "I've been thinking for some time it's time we brought a new member onto the board. What we need is a real leader. Someone who isn't afraid to take the bull by the horns. Someone with a real vision for what needs to happen."

"Someone we could talk into firing Miss Rudy," Lorraine added.

Owen Stout nodded. "Exactly."

"How about Sam Gardner?" Judy Iverson suggested. "Miss Rudy might be reluctant to harm a member of the clergy."

"Now there's a thought," Owen said.

"I make a motion to nominate Sam Gardner to the Library Board," Lorraine said.

"I'll second that motion," Judy said.

"All in favor, so signify by the raising of your hand," Owen said.

Three hands went up around the laundry table.

"That settles it," Owen said. "I'll ask him tomorrow."

He walked over to the meetinghouse the next morning. Sam was in his office. Owen sat down across from him. "Sam, the Library Board met last night, and we think a man with your leadership ability is just what we need for our board."

"No thanks," Sam said. "Not interested. I've got too much to do already."

"Well now, Sam, that's just what I told them, that you were too busy. But they said for me to ask you anyway, because you, being a minister and all, knew how important it was for people in the church to be active in their community and that you'd be eager to set a godly example for your congregation. You do want to set a godly example, don't you, Sam?"

And that's how Sam came to be the fourth member of the Library Board. The first meeting he attended, they elected him president. Then Owen made a motion that Miss Rudy be fired. It passed three votes to one. Then Lorraine Belcher made a motion that Sam be the one to tell her, which also passed three to one, which is how Sam found himself at the library one Wednesday evening in late May helping Miss Rudy get ready for the annual spring book sale.

He wasn't sure when he'd tell her she'd been let go, but when he walked into the basement and saw the boxes of donated books, he decided to wait until after she'd unpacked the boxes and priced the books.

It was just Miss Rudy and Sam. He did the lifting, while she marked the prices.

It took him an hour to work up the courage to ask her how long she'd been the librarian.

"Forty-three years," she said. "I was thirty-two when I moved here. I had a rather late start. My mother died and I had to take care of my father. I was their only child and they had me late in life. After Daddy died, I went to library school and here I am." She pointed to a stack of books. "Could you please set those books over here?"

Sam moved the books. "I bet you'll be glad when it's time to retire. It must be hard work keeping this library going."

Miss Rudy laughed. "Retire? Now why would I do that? What else is there for me? Books are all I have. No, I'll never retire. Oh my, Sam, look at this." She held up a book. "*Girl of the Limberlost* by Gene Stratton-Porter. I remember the first time I read this. I got it for my ninth birthday. My mother gave me her copy. I still have it."

She clutched it to her chest. "Sam, I know it's silly, but sometimes it feels like these books are the closest thing I have to a family."

"That's not silly, Miss Rudy."

"Thank you for saying so, Sam."

They unpacked more books.

"Sam, I have a question to ask you, and I need an honest answer."

"What is it, Miss Rudy?"

"The board's against me, aren't they?"

"I wouldn't say they're against you. They respect you a great deal."

Miss Rudy chuckled. "Oh, Sam, you're

such a diplomat. But I know what they're saying. That I'm too old, too set in my ways. That I can't raise money. Well, maybe that's true. But I never thought the purpose of a library was to show a profit. I always believed we had a higher calling."

"I guess times are changing, Miss Rudy."

"Well, I don't like it."

She pulled a book from the bottom of a box and read the title. "You might appreciate this, Sam. It's an old Bible."

She handed it to Sam. He read the cover. "The Queen Victoria Bible. Huh? I never heard of that Bible." He opened it to the first page. *"Printed in the Year of Our Lord 1851 by the Authority of Her Royal Highness Queen Victoria."*

Sam turned to the table of contents, then leafed through the book. "Where do you suppose it came from?"

"Probably someone's attic. We get a great number of books that way. You can have it if you want, Sam."

They spent another hour sorting books and marking prices, then called it a night. Sam walked Miss Rudy down the sidewalk to her home next to the library. She took his arm, leaning into him as they climbed the steps to her door. "Thank you for your help tonight, Sam."

"It was my pleasure. You take care now."

He walked home through the alley. He could see the lights on in the houses and people moving about. He thought about Miss Rudy, alone in her house, married to her books.

The phone rang as he came through his front door. It was Owen Stout. "So how'd she take it?"

"I didn't tell her."

"Aww, geez, Sam."

"I couldn't do it. Besides, I think she's doing a fine job."

"Sam, we've gone over that. We need someone who can raise money."

"She's having a book sale this weekend. That oughta help."

"Big money, Sam. We need big money."

The book sale was held that Saturday in the library basement. In the days before television, when people read more, the spring book sale was a big affair. People had to park in the funeral-home parking lot across the street. But these days, it's mostly Miss Rudy sitting in a folding chair in the basement, waiting for someone to show. The people who do come in talk with Miss Rudy about downloading books from the Internet and how one day there won't even be books. In twenty years, we won't even need libraries, they tell her. That's why she won't allow computers in the library. That, and the dirty pictures people would look at on the Internet.

Sam stopped by a little after nine. Miss Rudy poured him a glass of punch and offered him a cookie. "I made them myself. I thought if I had refreshments it might attract more people, but I guess not."

"It's still early, Miss Rudy. Don't give up yet."

He drank three cups of punch, ate nine cookies, and bought a book on antiques and collectibles. He sat next to Miss Rudy, thumbing through the book. "Boy, I can't believe how much some of this stuff is worth."

"Have you ever watched *Antiques Roadshow*?" Miss Rudy asked.

"Yeah, Barbara and I really like that show."

Flipping through the pages, the word *Victoria* caught Sam's eye. He turned back a page.

"Say, Miss Rudy, this is interesting. Remember that Bible you gave me? Here's a picture of one just like it."

He looked closer, then blinked his eyes and looked again.

"What's it say, Sam?"

"It says it's worth forty-eight thousand dollars."

He read further. "Only eleven known copies exist . . . Printed in 1851 . . . Had disappointing sales . . . All the surplus copies lost in a warehouse fire in 1852."

That was on Saturday. On Monday, Sam and Miss Rudy drove up to the city and on Wednesday phoned Owen Stout to tell him the spring book sale had generated forty-eight thousand, fifteen dollars and ninety-three cents. Then they called Bob Miles at the *Herald,* who brought his camera and took a picture of Miss Rudy and Sam standing in front of the library.

"So what's the story?" Bob asked. "How'd you raise so much money?"

Miss Rudy told him about the Queen Victoria Bible, how they'd sold it to a rare-books dealer for forty-eight thousand dollars. Bob didn't seem nearly as excited as they thought he'd be. Then again, it's hard to impress a journalist who's been at it as long as Bob.

"Yeah," Sam said, "the funny thing is that the board wants to let Miss Rudy go. Says she doesn't know how to raise money. Can you believe that? Maybe you oughta mention that in your article, Bob."

"Won't that get you in trouble with the board?" Bob asked.

"So what if it does. What's the worst

they'll do? Throw me off the board?"

Well, they wanted to, but they didn't. You don't just throw the Quaker minister off the Library Board. Not unless you want the members of the Friendly Women's Circle phoning your house asking what it is you have against the Christian faith. So they kept Sam, and they kept Miss Rudy, too.

She thought of retiring anyway, just to teach them a lesson, but then decided against it. How can a person retire when so much needs to be done? Instead, she took the money and hired Ernie Matthews to move the Ora Crandell Memorial Bookcase out of the ladies' rest room and set it across from the front door. She had the high-school art teacher make a clay bust of Ora Crandell. That was a little tricky since no one knew what Ora Crandell looked like. "Make her beautiful," Miss Rudy said. "I bet she had a beautiful soul, and I'm sure it showed in her face. Make her beautiful."

So the art teacher made her beautiful, and Miss Rudy displayed the bust on top of the memorial bookcase next to a plaque that read: *Ora Crandell, Pioneer Librarian — She Died That We Might Read.* It's the first thing people see when they come into the library.

Then, just to show she could keep up with the times, Miss Rudy bought four computers, hooked them up to the Internet, and posted a sign that read: *Persons Caught Looking at Dirty Pictures Will Have Their Names Published in the Newspaper.*

Because she is a Christian, she forgave the other board members. Because she is also a Quaker, she gave them a lecture first. Then she asked for a raise. "Somebody with my fund-raising experience can get twice as much somewhere else."

They raised her pay three thousand dollars, which Miss Rudy donated to the Librarian Hall of Fame in Topeka, Kansas.

"That'll teach 'em not to mess with librarians," she told Sam.

She had Uly Grant down at Grant's Hardware Emporium make a copy of the library key, which she gave to Sam. "Guard it with your life," she told him. "These books are more valuable than you could ever imagine."

All things considered, it hasn't been a good year for Bob Miles. Losing four million, forty-eight thousand dollars has quenched his zeal for life. Some people turn to God in times of trouble; Bob turned to the Coffee Cup Restaurant. He goes there each morning, around six-thirty, just as Heather Darnell is coming into work for the day.

He sits in the rear booth, his back to the wall, so he can watch Heather pour coffee and take breakfast orders. He orders three eggs, four pieces of bacon, a slice of ham, and an order of biscuits and gravy. From six-thirty to seven, it isn't all that crowded. Sometimes Heather sits across from him, and they visit.

Heather does most of the talking. She tells Bob about her boyfriend, how she doesn't think it'll work out, how he's only interested in one thing — basketball.

"I don't like basketball," Bob says. "Maybe I could be your boyfriend."

Heather laughs when he says that, like he's joking, even though he isn't. He dreams about Heather. He thinks of her while he's putting the newspaper together. He started a new feature in the *Herald* called "Folks Around Town." His idea was to take pictures of people working. But so far all the pictures he's run in the column have been of Heather — Heather pouring coffee, Heather serving up a plate of meat loaf, Heather tying on her apron at the start of the day, Heather re-stocking the salad bar with bacon bits and sunflower seeds.

"There are other people in this town besides Heather," his wife, Arvella, said one day.

Bob pretended he didn't hear her.

Then one afternoon in early June, after a long lunch at the Coffee Cup, he was sitting at his desk when he felt chest pains. He let out a little burp, which he thought might help, but it didn't. In fact, it made things worse. Now there was a tight pressure, like a band of steel cinched around him. He tried to remember the symptoms of a heart attack. He recalled something about numbness in the extremities. His arms did feel a little tingly. He broke out in a sweat, then felt chilled.

Arvella was in the back room.

"Arvella, come up here a minute, could you?"

By the time she got there, he was slumped in his chair.

It took twenty minutes for Johnny Mackey to get there with his ambulance and another thirty minutes to make it to the hospital in Cartersburg. The bad thing about the funeral-home owner driving the ambulance is that he has no incentive to hurry. Arvella rode in the back, holding on to Bob with one hand and smoothing his hair with the other. Tears were streaming down her face.

"Don't die, honey. Don't die. Don't leave me."

Looking up at her, Bob was wracked with guilt for ever thinking about Heather. How could I have even thought of another woman? he reflected. I need to ask Arvella's forgiveness.

"Arvella," he said in a weak voice.

"Yes, sugar."

"I need to ask your forgiveness for something I've done."

"No you don't. Everything'll be fine. You just worry about getting better." She kissed his forehead.

"I just want you to know that after I'm gone you might hear things about me and that Heather girl from the Coffee Cup. I just want you to know that you're the only woman I really ever loved."

Arvella reached down to hug him. "Oh, Bob, I love you, too. And don't you worry about what other people are saying. All that matters to me is that you get better."

Just then Johnny Mackey pulled up to the emergency entrance. The doors swung open, and two men lifted Bob out of the ambulance and wheeled him inside. They asked Arvella to sit in the waiting room. She called her sister, who came and sat with her. It took hours of testing to find out Bob hadn't had a heart attack after all. What he'd had was lunch at the Coffee Cup — two bowls of chili, three cups of coffee, and a piece of chocolate pie.

"Worst case of heartburn I've ever seen," the doctor told Arvella and her sister out in the waiting room. "We gave him some antacid, which ought to calm things down well enough for him to go home. Still, it's a good thing you brought him in. A man his age, you can't be too careful. It wouldn't hurt him to watch his diet and start exercising a little."

They finally let Arvella in to see him. He was propped up in bed, a slight grin on his face.

"I guess it was something I ate," he said.

"What's this you were telling me about you and Heather?"

"Oh, nothing, really." He tried to change the subject. "The doctor said I'll be able to go home just as soon as they get the paperwork filled out."

"Well, I'm leaving now," Arvella said. "My sister's here. She's going to give me a ride home."

"How'll I get home?"

"Why don't you give Heather a call. Maybe she can come and get you. You seem to be pretty good friends, after all."

He didn't call Heather. This wasn't the kind of thing he wanted getting around the

Coffee Cup. He called Sam Gardner instead. Sam was the only one he knew who wouldn't pry.

It was dark by the time Sam dropped Bob off in front of his house. The front door was locked, which was odd. They never locked their doors. Bob didn't even have a key. He walked around to the back door. It was locked, too. Arvella peered through the curtain on the door.

"Arvella, I'm home. Can you let me in? The door's locked."

"I know. I locked it."

"Aww, c'mon, Arvella, let me in."

"Maybe you can sleep at Heather's."

"Will you forget about Heather. We didn't do anything."

"Don't tell me that. I woke up a few weeks ago, and you weren't in the house. You were off with her. Don't lie and tell me different."

"I was out in the garage, Arvella."

"I've had it with your lies, Bob Miles."

He wanted to tell her about finding the time capsule and sawing it open out in the garage, but he figured that'd just make her more angry.

"Well, if you can't let me in, will you at least hand me out my car keys?"

"You know, Bob, the doctor said you need to exercise more, so why don't you walk?" Then she closed the curtain and walked away.

Bob sat on the porch swing, waiting for her to cool down. Around ten o'clock the downstairs lights in the house went off and the bedroom light went on. He stood out in the driveway, watching through the upstairs window as Arvella got ready for bed. A few minutes later, the bedroom fell dark.

Bob walked the four blocks to his office, where he slept on the floor. He walked back home the next morning. The doors were still locked, so he went to the Coffee Cup for breakfast. Heather was there. He didn't talk much, and it was busy so Heather didn't visit with him.

Dale Hinshaw sat down across from him. "I thought you were in the hospital. I heard from Johnny Mackey that you'd had a heart attack. What's goin' on?"

"No, they thought it was a heart attack, but it wasn't. I'm okay." He didn't tell Dale it'd only been indigestion.

"Say, Dale, can I borrow your car today. Mine's not working, and I need to go to the bank in Cartersburg."

"Well, sure, Bob. That's no problem, I guess." He handed Bob his car keys.

Bob settled up his bill, nodded good-bye to Heather, then climbed in Dale's Plymouth, fired it up, and drove to Cartersburg to the bank. He cashed in his thousand-dollar CD, then drove back to Harmony to Grant's Hardware Emporium.

The new refrigerators were lined up along the back wall. There weren't many to choose from. Uly handed him a catalog. "I can order anything in here and have it at your house next week."

Bob didn't think he could sleep on the office floor a whole week.

"You have anything you can deliver today?"

"Well, sure, Bob. We got these," he said, pointing to the refrigerators. "This one's a nice one. It has an ice maker. The ladies sure like those. And this here is an ice-water dispenser. You just press this little gizmo and cold water comes out."

"Say, that's nice. How much is it?"

"Nine and a quarter, plus tax. And we'll deliver it and hook it up for free and take away the old one."

"You got a deal."

Bob dropped Dale's car off and walked the five blocks home. He was sitting on the porch swing when Uly pulled up in his truck with the new refrigerator in back. Arvella was still locked inside the house. Bob tapped on the door.

"Go away, Bob."

"Honey, you'll need to open the door."

"Why?"

"So we can get our new refrigerator in."

Arvella peered through the window and saw the refrigerator. "You can't buy me off," she said.

"I'm not trying to," Bob said. "It's just my way of saying I'm sorry."

She was weakening.

"Does it have an ice maker?"

"Sure does. Plus a cold-water dispenser."

The door eased open. She looked at Bob. "What did you and Heather do?"

"Just talked, that's all, honey. I swear. Can I come home?"

"I better never hear of anything between you two, or that's it. I won't stand for it, Robert J. Miles."

"I understand," Bob said.

She opened the door and let him in. They emptied the food out of their old Kelvinator refrigerator, which Uly hauled outside. He and Bob wrestled the new refrigerator into place.

"Be careful, Bob," Arvella said. "Don't strain so. You know what the doctor said about heart attacks."

Uly hooked up the cold-water dispenser and showed them how to operate the ice maker. After he left, Bob and Arvella put their food in the new refrigerator, then had a glass of water out of the dispenser.

They were sitting at the kitchen table. It was the best Bob had felt in a whole month. He was flattered Arvella would actually think someone like Heather might be attracted to him. He had a paunch and was losing his hair. The shirt he was wearing was older than Heather. But to Arvella he was still the object of a young woman's desire.

He reached across the table and took her hand. "I hope you like your new refrigerator."

"You didn't have to do that, you know. Why'd you do that?"

"Because I didn't know what else to do. And because I love you. And to thank you for putting up with me."

She squeezed his hand, just a little, not too hard. "I thought I was going to lose you. I thought you were dying. I worry about you. You don't exercise and you eat food that isn't good for you."

"Maybe I shouldn't eat at the Coffee Cup so much," Bob said. "Maybe I should stay home and eat."

"I'd like that."

It was supper time. She fixed him Egg-Beater scrambled eggs, two turkey-sausage patties, and toast with oleo.

By the time he'd finished eating, the ice maker had made the first cubes. Bob poured two glasses of iced tea, and they went outside to sit on the porch swing. They rocked back and forth, not saying much, content with the quiet. After a while, Bob said, "You want to walk to the Dairy Queen and get an ice-cream cone?"

"How about some frozen yogurt instead?"

"Do they sell that at the Dairy Queen?"

"Yes. It's new. I saw it on their sign just the other day."

"Let's walk," Bob said. "I can use the exercise."

So that's what they did. They walked east on Marion Street to Washington Street, turned north at the Royal Theater and headed down Main Street to the Dairy Queen. They held hands, just like when they were teenagers and going on dates at the Royal Theater.

Bob thought about the four million, forty-eight thousand dollars he'd almost had. He thought of all the places he could have visited. But walking beside his beloved, holding her hand, with the crickets starting their evening song, he decided being home with Arvella was better.

Three

What Goes Around

School let out the last Friday in May, just before Memorial Day. The school isn't air-conditioned, so all the kids and teachers were glad for the year to end. It turned hot early, and even though they propped open the windows and the teachers brought fans from home, the varnish on the old desks was still sticky from the heat. Mr. Griswold, the janitor, had Uly Grant at the hardware store order an exhaust fan for the school attic, which he and Uly installed the week before school let out.

It was a big fan. It'd looked smaller in the catalog when they'd ordered it from a company in Chicago. They had to take it apart to get it up the narrow attic stairway, then reassemble it in the attic. It took them two days. They had to cut a hole in the roof, wire up the fan, then climb out on the roof to caulk around the opening. It was a beautiful late spring day. The heat had broken, and the sun was shining with an occasional puffy cloud drifting past. Mr. Griswold and Uly sat on the roof looking out over the town. If they looked to the south, they could see Asa and Jessie Peacock's new barn on the hill behind their house.

The schoolhouse is the highest building in Harmony, if you don't count the grain bin at the Co-op. It is three stories tall and was built in 1929 on the south end of Washington Street. The school was going to be four stories tall, but the Depression hit and the town ran out of money and had to stop at three stories. People moved to the city to look for work, and they didn't need four stories after all.

All the children in town attend there, though there's been talk of building a new school out on the edge of the town for the upper grades. It's always the new people who want to build a new school. They move here from other places, two or three families a year, and want to change things. It takes them a few years to learn that folks like things the way they are.

When they first come to town they attend the school-board meetings and talk about how the school they came from had a swimming pool and a better football field, even though the football field at the park works just fine and has since 1911 when Coach Leedy marked off the field and installed the first goalposts.

It's a lucky field. The single victory over Harmony's arch rival, the Cartersburg Carps, was accomplished on that field in 1958. The school took down the goalposts and cut them into one-foot lengths, which were given to the players. Mr. Griswold was the center on that team and he still has his section of goalpost, mounted on a board and hanging on the wall in his workshop next to the boiler in the school basement.

He and Uly could see the football field from the roof of the schoolhouse.

"Yeah," Mr. Griswold said, recalling their victory, "we wouldn't have won, except that the coach's wife cut out brown cloth in the shape of a football and sewed it on the front of our jerseys so it looked like we was all carrying the ball. They didn't know who to tackle and by the time they figured it out, we'd made a touchdown."

Uly laughed.

"Yeah, they threw a fuss about it. Said it was cheating, but they couldn't find anything against it in the rule book, and that's how we won."

"I bet that was something."

They fell quiet, looking at the clouds.

"Ain't it peaceful up here," Mr. Griswold said. "I like to come up here when the weather's nice and eat my lunch. Lots to see up here." He pointed up Washington Street. "That house with the red roof is Bea Majors's place. Last week, I seen her carry her trash over and put it in Hester Gladden's trash can when Hester wasn't home."

They ate their lunch, looking out over the town. Uly didn't say much. Mostly, he just listened. Being up that high reminded him of when he was a little boy and rode the Ferris wheel when the Happy Jack Carnival had come to town. He was maybe seven years old. It came the week after school let out, and his father, who was sober that day, had taken Uly to the carnival and let him go on the rides.

Uly liked the Ferris wheel most of all. They were on their third loop when the Ferris wheel broke down with Uly and his daddy in the top car. They were stuck up there for two hours. It turned dark while they were up there. All over town, they could see the streetlights blink on, one by one. It was the most time Uly had ever spent alone with his father.

At home his daddy would be watching TV, and Uly would say something and his father would say, "Don't bother me now, son. I wanna see this." But there wasn't any TV on the Ferris wheel, so they talked. At first Uly was a little scared. Then his daddy told him about how when he was Uly's age he'd been stuck on a Ferris for five whole days. "Yeah, it was something, and when they finally got me down, they had a big parade for me and gave me all the ice cream I could eat, and that was a lot of ice cream 'cause I hadn't eaten in five days. They even wrote a story about it in the newspaper. Now if you're brave like I was, I'll take you to the Dairy Queen when we get down from here and you can get anything you want."

He told Uly what the town was like when he was a boy growing up. "There was a train then and once a year, the week before Christmas, we'd ride the train up to the city to see the Christmas lights. We'd wear our nicest clothes. And if we were good, your grandma let us pick out a toy at Woolworth's. Maybe when we get down from here, I'll take you over to Kivett's and you can pick out a toy."

He told how, when he was a boy, he'd skip school the first nice day of spring and walk the two miles out to the Hodges' farm to go fishing. "That wasn't a big deal back then. You could do something like that and not get in trouble, but now you'd get in trouble.

Maybe this Saturday we can go fishing out there, just you and me."

He talked about how when he was little he would go to the movies at the Royal Theater. "Yeah, it cost a dime to get in back then. Jujubees was only a nickel, plus they gave you a free *Spy Smasher* comic book. It was during the war. They'd show the newsreels with all the soldiers."

Down below, they could see the men from the carnival working on the engine of the Ferris wheel. Exum Furbay, the volunteer fire chief, had left the fish-fry tent and was standing at the base of the Ferris wheel, every now and then yelling out for Uly and his father to stay put.

"The idiot. Where's he think we're gonna go?" Uly's dad said.

With the sun down, it turned chilly. Uly's dad took off his windbreaker and wrapped it around Uly. Then after a while they heard the engine pop, then catch, and they felt a lurch. Their seat rocked back and forth. "Here we go," Uly's dad said, as they advanced clockwise to the ground.

When they climbed off the Ferris wheel, Uly waited for his dad to take him to the Dairy Queen like he'd promised, but instead he took Uly home. Then he went to the Buckhorn and got drunk. Uly fell asleep on the couch waiting for him to come home. His mother carried him upstairs to bed. Uly was so hurt he didn't talk to his father for two weeks, but his father didn't even notice. So Uly just forgave him. When someone you love is an alcoholic, you have ample opportunities to forgive. Later that summer the Happy Jack Carnival went bankrupt, and there hadn't been a carnival in town since.

Some thirty years later, on the Memorial Day after school let out, two men in an old pickup worked their way through town nailing carnival posters to the telephone poles. The carnival rolled into town Thursday and set up on the town square. There was a Ferris wheel, which they erected in front of Grant's Hardware Emporium. The games of chance were arranged along Marion Street, from the Coffee Cup Restaurant east to the Johnny Mackey Funeral Home. The rest of the rides were assembled on Washington Street, alongside the library and Dairy Queen. The volunteer firefighters pitched their fish-fry tent in the empty lot between the Royal Theater and the Baptist church.

Not everyone was happy to see the carnival come to town. The Baptists were especially concerned when they parked the Snake Lady trailer on the street in front of their church.

On the side of the trailer was a painting of a woman with only a snake to obscure her feminine charms. Bernie, the policeman, had them move it over to the alley behind the *Harmony Herald* building. The Snake Lady, when she wasn't wearing snakes, wore dirty blue jeans and a black T-shirt, helped set up the carnival rides, and sold sno-cones.

The old Happy Jack Carnival used to stay a week, but this one lasted only three days. On Sunday evening, Uly Grant took his three little boys and walked uptown to the carnival. They rode the Scrambler and the merry-go-round; then he bought them sno-cones, which they ate while sitting on the bench in front of the library. They could just see the Ferris wheel rising over the top of the hardware store.

"Did I ever tell you about the time me and your grandpa got stuck on the Ferris wheel? It was something. We were up there for two hours."

They took a loop on the Ferris wheel. When they reached the top, it stopped, just for a moment, just long enough for them to look out over the town. They could see the school and the football field and their house a few blocks south of the square. The sun was setting. Over on Mill Street, a streetlight blinked on. Then the Ferris wheel lurched and around they went.

Uly's been sober two years. His father is in his late sixties now and still drinks. Spends most of his evenings at the Buckhorn on the stool at the far end of the bar. He's a quiet drinker, doesn't visit much with the other men. Just sits on his stool and drinks, every now and then raising his head to watch the ball game, then having another drink. Sometimes, in the early afternoon, he stops past the hardware store, but Uly pretty much runs the place.

Uly was following in his father's footsteps. What saved him were his three little boys. Not wanting to disappoint them. Not wanting to make promises he wouldn't keep. Not wanting them to be ashamed when the other kids laughed about how their old man was a drunk. So he went to AA in the Harmony Friends basement and stopped drinking. He still goes every Wednesday night. He's not sure how it works, whether he'll have to go every week for the rest of his life. A day at a time, he tells himself.

A couple nights a week, Uly's phone rings late at night. It'll be Bill from the Buckhorn, calling Uly to come get his father. Uly drives down in his truck, loads up his dad, takes him home, puts him in the shower, then puts him to bed.

"You shouldn't do that," Uly's wife says. "When are you going to be done with him?"

But all Uly can think about it was how when he was little his daddy took him to the carnival and took him on the Ferris wheel. When you have a father who's broken every promise he ever made, but you still want to love him, you look for the smallest good in him. How he gave you his jacket when it turned cold. How when you were scared, he held you close.

"There are things in him worth loving," Uly told his wife.

He had once asked Bill at the Buckhorn not to serve him anymore. Bill said, "It won't work. He'd just drive over to Cartersburg and do his drinking. At least here he won't hurt nobody."

Uly read somewhere that alcoholism might be genetic. He hopes it isn't true. He worries for his sons, that they might go that way. He takes them to church every Sunday and in the quiet time he prays for God to protect them. He's cut back his hours at the store to be with the boys. They play pitch and catch in the side yard, and on Saturday evenings he and his wife walk them to the Dairy Queen.

When Uly has a problem with one of his

boys and doesn't know what to do, he grows resentful at all the things his father should have taught him, but never did. Still, in the back of his mind is the recollection of how one night, in early summer, for two hours on top of a Ferris wheel, his father did exactly the right thing. So when his boys are scared, Uly tells them stories to help them be brave. And when they're cold, he gives them his jacket and draws them close. The rest of the stuff he does by the seat of his pants, hoping he won't mess things up too bad.

The week after school let out, he walked with his boys down to the schoolhouse, unlocked the back door with the key Mr. Griswold keeps hidden behind the downspout, and took them up to the roof. They watched Bea Majors sneak her garbage out and put it in Hester Gladden's trash can. They watched the moon rise over the lucky football field. Then it turned chilly, so they came down from the roof, passed through the church-quiet halls of the school, and walked home down Mill Street.

There are things we see with our eyes, sitting high and looking out. And there are things we see with our hearts, sitting still and looking in.

Four
Deena

With warm weather here, business has fallen off at Deena Morrison's Legal Grounds Coffee Shop. In the winter, people come in, sit by the fire, drink their coffee, and visit, but in warm weather they shift their allegiance to Oscar and Livinia Purdy at the Dairy Queen. With business slowing down, Deena has been thinking of closing the Legal Grounds the first week of June and taking a vacation. Her grandmother Mabel told her about the tanned young men in the Caribbean, and Deena thinks she might go there, meet one, get married, and bear his children before she gets any older.

Deena had been planning on marrying Wayne Fleming after his wife, Sally, left him. Then Sally came home and told Wayne she had leukemia, and he took her back. She got herself healed, ostensibly by the Reverend Johnny LaCosta of the Johnny LaCosta Worship Center, and Wayne and Sally put their marriage back together. Everyone's glad for them, even Deena, though it's hard not to be bitter.

Deena still attends church at Harmony Friends Meeting, having read in "Dear Abby" that if you want to find a good man you should go to churches, not bars. With the healing of Sally Fleming now fully accomplished, the Friendly Women's Circle has taken on the marriage of Deena Morrison as their latest project. To that end, Fern Hampton invited Deena to dinner so she could introduce her to her nephew Ervin, something she failed to mention to Deena. Fern sat Deena next to Ervin, then regaled her with stories of his meteoric rise through the street department.

"Ervin's moving right up the ladder. He's only been there six years, and he's already in charge of the manhole covers."

"Thirty-three manhole covers in this town," Ervin boasted. "And I know where every single one is."

"Amazing," Deena said. "Absolutely amazing. How do you do it?"

"A good memory is all it takes. You just got to train your mind," Ervin said. "But there are days when the pressure can get to you."

"I can imagine."

She wasn't sure what to say after that, so she smiled, ate as quick as she could, turned down dessert, yawned at six-thirty, and said it was time to call it a day.

Fern suggested Ervin walk her home. "A lady can't be too careful these days. That's the nice thing about having a big, strong man by your side. Here, Deena, feel Ervin's muscle." She placed one of Deena's hands on Ervin's biceps. "That's what comes from lifting manhole covers all day. And yet, feel how gentle his hands are." She placed Deena's other hand in Ervin's hand. "Oh, it does my heart good to see two handsome people in the bloom of youth. Enjoy your walk, kids."

Deena wasn't sure what to talk with Ervin about when he walked her home. "Dear Abby" always said to talk about a man's interests, but she didn't know much about manhole covers.

"So, Ervin, how did you come to be in charge of the manhole covers?"

"Just lucky, I guess. I tell you, Deena, manhole covers are a lot more complicated than most folks realize. But people don't even give them a second thought. They just think they'll always be there when they need them. They just drive right over 'em. People sure are gonna be surprised some day when

71

they wake up and all the manhole covers are gone, I tell you that right now."

"That's a good point, Ervin. I must say I've never given it much thought myself."

"A lot of people are that way. They're book smart, but they don't have any common sense. Take me for instance, I've never been to college, but I know a whole lot more than people who've got two or three college degrees. Here I am, only twenty-four years old and already in charge of all the manhole covers."

"That's certainly impressive," Deena agreed. "Oh, look, I'm home. Thank you for the walk, Ervin. It was a pleasure to meet you."

He stopped past the next three evenings to ask her for a walk. She thanked him, but told him she didn't feel well. Fern collared her at church the next Sunday. "You know, someone who's sick as much as you are ought to have good health insurance. Did Ervin ever mention his benefits at the street department?"

Deena is weary of the pressure. Besides trying to find her a husband, the Friendly Women have been hinting that it's time she joined their venerable organization. Back in April, a group from the Circle visited and invited her to join so she could help make noodles for their annual Chicken Noodle Dinner.

"I'd love to be in the Circle," she told them. "But you only meet in the daytime and I work then. If you met in the evening, I could join you."

Fern Hampton smiled a pinched smile and said in a tight voice, "Now, Deena dear, you have to be flexible. We've been meeting in the daytime since our beginning. We can't change our meeting time just to accommodate one person. That wouldn't be fair, would it?"

"I don't see why we can't meet evenings," Gloria Gardner said. "There are quite a few young women at the meeting who work days. We retired folks can meet anytime. I think we need to accommodate the younger women."

They've had this same talk once a month for the past ten years. The noodle makers are dying off, and the younger women aren't stepping up to the plate. They don't want to make noodles. They want to open a food pantry or attend a women's Bible study. Noodle making is not high on their list of priorities.

Fern believes it's a spiritual matter, that if the younger women loved the Lord, they'd quit their day jobs and make noodles with the Friendly Women.

The younger women don't like the Chicken Noodle Dinner. It's too much work for the small amount of money they raise. When the Friendly Women visited her, Deena had suggested they hold an auction.

"I think an auction is a wonderful idea," Gloria Gardner said.

Fern Hampton squirmed in her chair. "An auction? I'm not sure about that. That doesn't seem very dignified."

Fern has annoyed so many of the women for so long, that when they sensed her discomfort with an auction, they championed the idea and scheduled it for the first Saturday in June. This turned Fern against Deena, who had not only spurned her nephew Ervin, but obviously didn't respect Fern's counsel on such matters.

Fern was willing to forgive those transgressions until Deena, who wasn't even a member of the Circle, barged in, without permission, and solicited donations for the auction. She talked Harvey Muldock into offering a tune-up at his garage. The Kroger gave a canned ham. Kyle at the barbershop donated a shave. Oscar and Livinia at the Dairy Queen contributed a dozen Dilly Bars. Dale Hinshaw gave a lawn mower that only needed one wheel, and Bea Majors volunteered a free evening of organ music.

Deena offered to prepare a free dinner for two at the Legal Grounds, candlelight and soft music included.

There is a sad lack of romantic opportunities in Harmony, which Deena believes is the reason she's still single. They have couples bowling on Saturday nights at the Country Lanes. There's Italian Night at the Coffee Cup on Wednesday nights, but it isn't all that inspiring — Chef Boyardee spaghetti from a can and Bea Majors on the organ.

The Circle held the auction in the meetinghouse basement. It was crowded, there not being anything else to do in town. Fern came with her nephew Ervin. Though Fern had initially resisted the auction, she couldn't bear to see something happen without her having a say, so she came on board and declared herself in charge of the evening. She stood at the lectern, moving through the list of items, trying to talk fast like a real auctioneer. She didn't have a gavel, so she used a meat-tenderizing mallet instead. She'd just sold off the canned ham when Deena slipped out to use the rest room. It was just the opportunity Fern had been looking for. "The next item up for bid is dinner with Deena Morrison."

Many of the men present wanted to bid

on a dinner with Deena Morrison, but their wives wouldn't have approved. Ervin was the only bachelor present. "Five dollars," he shouted.

"Going, going, gone to my nephew Ervin for five dollars!" *Bang!* went Fern with her meat-tenderizing mallet, as quick as she could, before Deena returned.

Dinner with Ervin was not what Deena had in mind, which she pointed out to Fern afterward. "It wasn't dinner *with* me. It was a dinner for two *prepared* by me."

"Well, now, Deena dear, I'm sure if you want to prepare the meal, that'll be just fine with Ervin."

But what upset Deena most of all was that she had gone for only five dollars and that Bea Majors and her organ playing had gone for fifty.

"Five dollars," she told her grandmother Mabel. "Well, it's good to know what I'm worth. I have a law degree, own a successful business, have been told I'm reasonably attractive, and I go for five dollars while Bea Majors goes for fifty. I don't know why I stay in this town."

Deena has always been a disciple of positive thinking, but lately it's been a difficult philosophy to sustain. She sits in church and watches the mothers with their children and aches to have a family. The worst Sundays are when Pastor Sam dedicates a baby. She doesn't even go on those Sundays anymore.

Another voice in her says she doesn't need to be a wife or a mother to be happy, but that voice is growing quieter. She wants to love and be loved. When she was a little girl, she'd dream about who she'd marry. She had an idea of what he'd look like. But now she's flexible, more willing to revise her image of the perfect husband, which is why she ended up going out to dinner with Ervin after all.

The next Friday night, they drove to Cartersburg to the Masonic Lodge's catfish buffet. Ervin complained about his job at the street department the whole time. "It's the politics I don't like. The boss's nephew started a year after me and they already got him in charge of painting sidewalk curbs. Now you tell me if that's right. That don't seem right to me."

He tried to hold her hand across the pile of catfish bones, but she sat with her hands in her lap. When it came time to pay the check, Ervin said, "Well, I guess this is on you, seein's how the dinner was your donation to the auction."

Deena paid, and they got in Ervin's car and pulled out onto the highway. Ervin went home the long way, through the country. He drove slowly, every now and then point- ing out a place of interest. He draped his arm across the backrest, his fingers scant inches from Deena's shoulder. The car rolled to a stop.

Oh, Lord, please don't let him try to kiss me, she prayed. Then she got mad. If he thinks a five-dollar bid entitles him to a kiss, he's crazy. He might have won the dinner, but dessert was not included.

"Care for a breath mint?" he asked. "It'll get rid of the fish taste."

"No, thank you." Right now, the fish taste was her best defense.

She wondered what she should do if he tried to kiss her. She'd read in "Dear Abby" that it was best to say no in a firm voice. Don't be passive, "Dear Abby" warned. Hold your head up, look him in the eye and say, "NO!"

Ervin reclined his car seat. She could sense his hand moving across her headrest, like a spider inching closer.

"You have pretty hair," he said.

"Thank you."

"Of course, long hair isn't good for bath- room drains. It clogs 'em up something ter- rible. If we get together, you should maybe get it cut."

Her stomach rumbled. She thought it was her nerves, but she wasn't sure. Maybe it was the fish. She could still taste it. Her mouth felt watery. She needed to spit. Her stomach rumbled again. There wasn't time to roll down her window, so when Ervin leaned in for a kiss, she threw up on him instead.

The rest of the way home Ervin drove considerably quicker. Deena apologized. He said it was okay, but she could tell by the way he set his mouth that it wasn't okay. He dropped her off in front of her house. He didn't even open her car door — he just sat there while she got out of the car, then drove off with scarcely a good-bye.

As for Deena, she was feeling better. Her mother had always said vomiting made a person feel better, and she was right. Deena felt much improved. She went inside, brushed her teeth, and took a shower. It was too early to go to bed, so she put on a fresh change of clothes and went for a walk through town.

She wondered if she should write Ervin a letter of apology for throwing up on him, then decided against it. That's what he gets for bidding only five dollars, she told herself. I'm worth more than five dollars. He should apologize to me. Stopping the car to kiss me — what nerve! Who does he think he is? Who does he think I am?

The next morning, she went to the Legal Grounds Coffee Shop early to bake muffins. A little after seven, Fern Hampton stopped in. "Oh, I see you're feeling better. Ervin said you weren't feeling well. He said you were feeling so bad he had to help you into the house. I tell you, Deena dear, there aren't many gentlemen left like him anymore. Don't you just want to be with him forever?"

Deena held her head up, looked Fern in the eye, and said, "No!"

Fern gave a pinched smile. "Now, Deena dear, don't be hasty. After all, you're not getting any younger. A girl in your situation can't afford to be picky."

"I'm not interested. Now could I get you some coffee?"

"No, thank you," Fern said crisply, as she turned and marched out of the Legal Grounds.

It was early yet. Deena poured a mug of coffee, sat down, and remembered how Wayne Fleming used to come to the shop about this time of day, before the customers arrived. They would talk, she and Wayne, and laugh and hold hands. She misses that. She didn't think she would, but she does.

When she sits in the meetinghouse on Sunday mornings and sees his wife lean into him, she misses it. On mornings like this, when everyone else in town has someone to sit across from and she doesn't, she misses it.

A silent prayer formed itself in her mind. Lord, I am so lonely. Please send someone into my life who will love me, who I can love back.

Some people think Deena's a snob, that she regards herself too highly. She is picky, that is true, but she believes pickiness is just another word for discernment. She would rather be alone than married to a man who thought an evening with her was worth only five dollars. She feels a strong obligation not to diminish her gene pool with the likes of Ervin.

One of the Friendly Women gave her a book on how to be a submissive wife, which she pitched in the trash. She doesn't want a boss; she wants a husband. But not just any husband — one she can love and respect, who'll love and respect her back. Someone she can sit across the table from on Saturday mornings and hold hands. Someone who, when supper is finished, would dry and put away while she washed. Someone who might read the *Herald* and say, "Well, would you look at that. The Friendly Women are

having an auction this Saturday. Let's go."
And if he went, and her name came up, he
would bid all the money he had to be with
her.

Five
The Furnace Committee

The meeting of the Furnace Committee was held the last Tuesday in June, Dale Hinshaw presiding. The committee was formed in the late 1990s to purchase and install a new furnace in the Harmony Friends meetinghouse. Everyone assumed the committee would disband with the new furnace in place, but Dale has kept it going. They meet once a month to inspect the furnace, change the filters, and fire the burners. That takes about fifteen minutes, after which they set up a card table in the church basement and play poker for matchsticks. There is a long list of men waiting to serve on the Furnace Committee.

Their wives wonder why it's necessary to check on the furnace so often and sometimes question their husbands. In defense of their furnace ministry, the men clip articles from the newspaper about entire families dying of carbon monoxide poisoning from bad furnaces. They cut out stories of houses burning to the ground and firemen saying, "We're not quite sure, but it looks like the fire started in the furnace." Once, they found an article about a church in Michigan whose furnace blew up *during* the worship service; a deacon was burned and nearly died. The Furnace Committee clipped that article and had Frank, the secretary, run it in the church newsletter along with the caption, *This would never have happened in a church with a Furnace Committee!!!* That kept their wives quiet a whole year.

They play cards for about three hours — Dale Hinshaw, Harvey Muldock, Asa Peacock, and Ellis Hodge. They talk about fishing and tell jokes and discuss certain people in the church who aren't quite as holy as everyone thinks. It's about the only time Dale Hinshaw is bearable. The rest of the time he's a little too pious to suit the other three, but on Furnace Committee night he leaves his Bible at home.

They talk about their children. Ellis Hodge talks about Amanda, whom he and Miriam adopted from his no-good brother, Ralph. She's in the eighth grade and is playing on a traveling girls' softball team this summer, which perplexes Ellis, but he goes along with it.

Asa Peacock has two children, both of

whom are grown and live out of state. Dale and Dolores Hinshaw have three sons, Raymond Dale, Harold Dale, and Robert Dale.

"So, Harvey, how are your kids?" Dale asked at the June meeting of the Furnace Committee.

"Oh, they're fine. Susie's expecting again. Number four. Denise's husband, Henry, just got promoted. He's the foreman now. Bought hisself a new bass boat last week. We're going fishing next month."

"How's your boy doing?" Dale asked.

"All right, I guess. He was home last week for a visit."

"Is he married yet?"

"Nope, not yet." Then Harvey changed the subject, even though Dale had more questions he'd wanted to ask about Harvey's son.

Harvey's son is James. They call him Jimmy. Harvey has never really understood him. Jimmy makes sculptures out of scrap metal, watches foreign movies, and sews his own clothes. Harvey likes Norman Rockwell, watches old World War II movies, and wears Dickie pants and shirts that he buys at the Co-op. There's not much common ground, and Harvey sometimes wonders if Jimmy is even his child, except they look a lot alike.

Jimmy doesn't come home much. He drives down for a short visit the week after Christmas and comes home for a long weekend every June. Harvey and Eunice don't even try to buy him anything for Christmas. They used to buy him flannel shirts, but when they visited him in Chicago, they found the shirts still in their wrappers in the bottom drawer of his dresser. Now they just give him money in a card.

When Jimmy was in high school, Eunice came home one day and found him in his bedroom crying. When she asked him what the matter was, he wouldn't say, but she finally got it out of him that he thought something was wrong with him, that he had certain feelings for other boys. He begged her not to tell Harvey, so she hasn't.

But being a mother, she had to do something, so she took Jimmy to talk with Pastor Taylor, who was the minister back then at Harmony Friends Meeting. No one had ever told Pastor Taylor anything like this, so he wasn't sure what to do either. Pastor Taylor preferred the old days, when people didn't feel compelled to tell a pastor their secrets. Some things he didn't want to know. He said a little prayer for Jimmy, then suggested maybe Jimmy go hunting and fishing a little more and things would turn out all right.

"You probably just haven't met the right girl," Pastor Taylor said.

When Jimmy went away to college, Eunice would pray he'd bring a nice girl home some weekend, but he never did. Then when he graduated from college, he moved to Chicago and has lived there ever since.

On his last trip home, he'd suggested to his mother maybe it was time to tell his dad he was gay, but Eunice wouldn't hear of it. "I wish you wouldn't," she said. "It will only hurt him and he won't understand. I know your father. He'll think it's his fault. I don't think you ought to come out of the attic just yet."

"It's coming out of the closet, Mom, not coming out of the attic."

Jimmy was secretly relieved not to have to tell his father. He had talked about it with a therapist, who had recommended he tell Harvey. It had sounded like a good idea in the therapist's office, three hundred miles from his father. But when he was sitting across from his dad at the kitchen table in late June, it didn't seem like a good idea after all, so he kept quiet.

The thing is, Harvey has suspected for

some time that Jimmy might be gay. He isn't married, he's never had a girlfriend, and he isn't a Catholic priest, so he must be gay, Harvey reasoned. But he's never said anything to Eunice. He doesn't want to hurt her. She wouldn't understand. She would blame herself, thinking maybe she had something to do with his being that way.

Harvey thought about telling Jimmy he knew. Whenever they're together, he can sense Jimmy is uncomfortable. They talk about other people in town and what the Odd Fellows Lodge is up to, but never about anything personal. There's a wall between them, an unspoken barrier that prevents such intimacy.

No one in town talks about these things, except for Dale Hinshaw, who feels compelled to share his opinion with anyone who'll listen. At the last meeting of the Furnace Committee, Dale told about an article on homosexuality in the *Mighty Men of God* newsletter. "Basically, they're that way because they want to be. They could change if they wanted to. They talked with some guys who were that way, and they got married and now they're just fine."

"I'm sure that's been true for some people," Ellis Hodge said, "but I don't think that's true for every gay person. I think it's more complex than that."

"Humph, that's what the liberals want ya t' believe," Dale said. "They won't let the truth out."

"You know, Dale, not everything is a liberal conspiracy," Asa Peacock said.

It troubles Dale that so many members of the Furnace Committee have been led astray. "I guess I can't blame 'em," he told his wife. "They're only hearing what the liberal media wants 'em to hear."

He wrote to the *Mighty Men of God* newsletter and bought gift subscriptions for the Furnace Committee. "Thank God there's still one magazine that'll tell the truth," he told his wife.

The official position of the *Mighty Men of God* newsletter is that gay people are going to hell, and anyone who doesn't think so is also going to hell. There's not much wiggle room in their theology, which Dale appreciates. Dale thinks the big problem in America is that there is too much wiggle room and not enough "Thus sayeth the Lord!" As long as he's in charge of the Furnace Committee, there'll be no truce with sin, he told his wife.

So Harvey never talks with Dale about Jimmy. He worries enough about his son without hearing Dale prophesy his eternal damnation. Before he figured out Jimmy was gay, Harvey knew what he thought about homosexuals. But now that his son is one, he's not so sure. He wishes he could talk with Eunice about it, but he can't bear the thought of her knowing.

He thought about talking with Pastor Sam to find out his opinion. But he supposed Sam would have to stick to the party line and be against it, elsewise Dale would get him fired. No, he didn't want to drag Sam into this. Sam had enough problems without Dale hounding him.

Harvey is not a man prone to philosophizing, but lately he's been wondering why it is that the angriest and loudest people are the ones who get their way in the church. When he first started going to church, back when the kids were little, he thought it was supposed to work the other way, that the kind and wise people were the ones who were listened to, but it isn't that way at all. It's the angry ones that get their way. Everyone else is afraid to buck them; they just kind of go along.

Like when they were putting in the furnace. Dale wanted the church to hire his son, Robert Dale, to install the furnace, even though that wasn't Robert Dale's line of work. But Robert Dale was between jobs and needed the money.

Ellis Hodge had said, "Dale, don't get me wrong, I like Robert Dale, but I'm not sure he's the one to do this. I think we ought to hire a professional. It might even be against the law for your son to do it, since he isn't licensed."

"Well, I never heard of such foolishness," Dale had said. "Here we are, letting the government tell us how to run the church."

"I didn't mean it that way, Dale. I'm just not sure Robert Dale is qualified. That's all I meant."

Dale lectured them about freedom of religion and helping those in need and how Robert Dale was in need. Finally the Furnace Committee caved in and let him do it.

Robert Dale bungled the job. He put the thermostat in the pastor's office two feet above a hot-air vent. To get the meeting room up to sixty-eight degrees, they have to turn the thermostat to eighty-eight. Sam's office is like a sauna. He has to open the windows, which defeats the purpose of having a furnace in the first place. Dale insists his son did nothing wrong, that that's the way it's supposed to work. He won't let a furnace man look at it, and since he's in charge of the Furnace Committee, he pretty well gets his way. Harvey doesn't understand that, but resisting Dale would take too much energy, energy Harvey doesn't have.

He's been spending time at the library with Miss Rudy, the librarian. She's been teaching him how to use the Internet. He wanted to find out all he could about homosexuality and figured that would be an anonymous way to do it. But the word *homosexual* has the word *sex* in it, so when Harvey typed it in, a beeper in the computer began screeching and the computer froze up. This was Miss Rudy's method of upholding community standards. Everyone in the library turned to look at Harvey.

"Harvey Muldock, what kind of filth are you up to?" Miss Rudy called out from her stool at the front desk.

Harvey panicked. "Nothing. I don't know what happened." He began striking various keys to silence the beeper, to no avail. Miss Rudy came out from behind the desk and peered at the computer screen. Her face reddened and she let out a gasp.

"Can you make it stop beeping like that?" Harvey yelled above the noise.

Miss Rudy tapped a key, and the beeper stopped. She glared at Harvey. "I won't have that smut in this library," she said.

"It's not what it looks like," he said. "I just wanted to look something up."

The next thing Harvey knew he was in Miss Rudy's office, telling her about Jimmy. He made her promise not to tell anyone, especially not his wife. "It'd break her heart," he said. "She'd think it was her fault. I just wanted some information, that's all. I don't know much about it, and I don't know who to ask."

So Miss Rudy taught Harvey how to use the Internet, and he has been reading up on the topic. He learned the various theories about the cause of homosexuality, ranging from man's sinful nature to a person's genetic code. Harvey suspects it's all tied to religion. If you attend a church where the pastor preaches about the seven-headed beast of Revelation, you lean toward the man's-sinful-nature theory. If your pastor has ever called God "Mother" or talked about "our brother, the whale," you likely favor the genetics hypothesis.

The Internet didn't help much. Harvey's still confused. The only thing he knows for sure is that he loves his son. He hopes God loves him, too. He isn't sure. Just when he's inclined to trust God's love, Dale Hinshaw says something that causes him to doubt it. Harvey wonders how Dale can know so much. To hear Dale tell it, you would think he was the only one the Lord ever spoke to.

Harvey finally worked up the courage to ask Ellis Hodge what he thought about gay people one evening after a meeting of the Furnace Committee.

"I heard a preacher on TV say God hates people like that, that he sends them to hell. Do you think that's so?" Harvey asked Ellis.

Ellis chuckled. "If it is, I want my offering money back." He laid a hand on Harvey's shoulder. "Harvey, an awful lot of folks hate anything and anyone they don't understand. That don't mean they're right."

"So let's say you had a son, and you found out he was that way. What would you do about it?" Harvey asked.

Ellis pondered that for a moment. "I think I would tell him I loved him. I suspect he'd want to hear that."

They checked the furnace one last time, shut off the lights in the church, and went out to the parking lot. Ellis climbed in his truck to drive home.

Harvey walked home. He looped around the block a couple extra times. He needed time to think. He said a little prayer for Jimmy. That helped. It always had. He thought back to when Jimmy was little and he'd take him to church. How they'd sit side by side, Harvey resting his hand on top of Jimmy's head, every now and then looking down at him and smiling with a fatherly pride. If the sermon went long, they'd pass notes back and forth on the church bulletins. For whatever reason, Harvey had saved them in the top drawer of his dresser. Whenever he reaches in for socks, he sees Jimmy's little-boy writing.

He wouldn't see Jimmy until Christmas. Six months away. Maybe instead of waiting that long to tell him he loved him, he could write him a note, maybe on the back of a church bulletin. They had some experience with notes, after all. Harvey thought about that. Yes, it seemed like a fine idea. Writing a note to your son saying you love him. Just a little note. "I love you, son. Can't wait to see you at Christmas. P.S. Your mother loves you, too."

Harvey still wasn't sure what he thought about homosexuality, but he did know he loved his son, and that seemed as fine a place to start as any.

Six

A Mighty Man of God

Dale Hinshaw knew it was a sign from the Lord when he found the spent helium balloon lying on the ground next to his garage back in early May. A piece of paper was tied to the balloon with the words, *If found, please contact Missy Griffith of Owasa, Iowa.* Underneath Missy's name was a phone number, which Dale called late that night, when the rates were cheapest.

Missy Griffith, it turns out, had been studying wind currents in her fourth-grade science class, and her teacher had the kids release helium balloons to see how far they would travel.

Dale had looked for Owasa in his atlas, but couldn't find it. "Just where is Owasa, exactly?" he asked Missy.

"Ten miles east of Buckeye," she said. "That's where we grocery shop."

That didn't help much, but Dale finally found it on his map. They calculated that

Missy's balloon had flown four hundred and twenty miles in three days.

"It might have got here earlier," Dale said. "I was gone yesterday, to the Mighty Men of God Conference up in the city. It might have come when I was up there."

"You're the farthest person to call," she told Dale. Dale felt a proud thrill.

A couple weeks later, a big envelope post-marked Owasa landed in Dale's mailbox. There was a newspaper in the envelope, and on the front page was a picture of Missy Griffith holding a map showing the distance from Owasa to Harmony. In the third paragraph, it mentioned Dale's name and how he'd found Missy's balloon next to his garage on a Thursday morning, though the article allowed as how it might have landed in Dale's yard on Wednesday when Dale was at the Mighty Men of God Conference in the city.

The thing was, the conference had ended with a plea for the Mighty Men of God to go out and make disciples of all the nations. Then, the very next day, Dale had found the balloon, which he took to be a sign from the Lord that he, Dale Hinshaw, was being called to launch the salvation balloons ministry.

Dale had been casting about for a new

way of spreading the Word after his Scripture eggs ministry had gone belly up when all his chickens had died of a poultry disease on Good Friday. Dale's Scripture eggs ministry had begun when Dale read in *Ripley's Believe It or Not* of a chicken who'd laid an egg with a scrap from a telephone book preserved in the yolk. That was when he'd had the idea to feed Scripture verses to chickens, who would then lay Scripture eggs, which Dale would distribute to unbelievers.

Things went well until Good Friday, when the Lord removed his hand of blessing and all the chickens died of a fearsome disease. Dale had been praying for a new ministry, and then had awakened to find the balloon in his yard the day after the Mighty Men of God Conference.

"It's not just a coincidence," he told his wife. "This is the Lord's doin'. I just know it. Why else would that balloon have landed in our yard?"

Dale's idea was to write the plan of salvation on a piece of paper, tie it to a helium balloon, and set it free when the wind was blowing toward heathen lands. The genius of the idea was in its simplicity. No more chickens in the basement to feed, no more poultry diseases to worry about, no more egg delivery to concern himself with. Just blow up the balloons, tie on the plan of salvation, set them free, and trust the Lord to direct them to heathen unbelievers.

It took the better part of May and June to save the money for a helium tank. He had gone to the May meeting of the elders to ask for two hundred dollars to get his balloon ministry off the ground. He showed the elders a map of the wind patterns, pointing out how, if he released the salvation balloons in Harmony, they would fly east toward all the liberals.

Miriam Hodge sat wondering why she had agreed to be an elder for another three years. "Why exactly do you need the money, Dale?"

"Mostly for a helium tank. I can buy the balloons myself, but I can't swing a helium tank just yet."

"I don't know," Sam Gardner said. "I don't think this is something the church would want to get behind. I think maybe we should pass on this one."

Dale tried not to hold it against them, but it was difficult. "It's like the Bible says," he told his wife, "where there is no vision, the people perish. They're dying — they just don't know it."

"You can thank the liberals for that," she said. "They've made it a crime to even pray.

No wonder the Christians are running scared."

With the church running scared, Dale saved his money and in early July bought a helium tank. He inflated two hundred balloons with the plan of salvation tied on each one. He had to use a lot of abbreviations to make the plan of salvation fit on a piece of paper, but he thought people could still understand it.

1. *ADMT U R A SNR.*
2. *TRN FRM SIN.*
3. *BELEV JESUS SAVZ SNRS.*
4. *INVIT JESUS N2 YR LIFE.*

Then he wrote his name and phone number at the bottom so people would call him.

It took the better part of a day to blow up the balloons. Two hundred balloons don't look like a lot when they're up in the sky, but when you have to blow them up yourself, it's a sizable number. Plus, writing out the plan of salvation two hundred times was no small feat. Then he worried that someone who couldn't read might find a salvation balloon, so he recorded several cassette tapes of the plan of salvation and tied them to balloons.

When he finished, the wind was blowing from the west at a steady ten miles an hour.

"They'll be in Washington, D.C., in a little over two days," he told his wife, then opened the garage door and pushed them out and up into the sky. The balloons rose in the air, a rainbow of color. A few stuck in the oak tree in the neighbor's yard, but most of them cleared the tree and headed east, toward the heathens.

That was on a Saturday. The next day at church he stood up during the prayer time and asked for prayers for his salvation balloons, that the Lord would direct them to unbelievers.

"I can't help but think the Lord had them blowing toward Washington, D.C., for a reason," he said. "Maybe some of our leaders will find one and be saved, and this nation will come back to the Lord."

"Amen to that," said Bea Majors from the organ.

For the hundredth time in the two years he'd been there as pastor, Sam Gardner wished he were somewhere else.

Dale wiped away a tear. "I feel so privileged to do the Lord's work this way," he sniffed. "I'll be releasing four hundred balloons this Saturday. I'll need some help.

They're predicting winds from the south, which should carry the balloons toward Chicago. Now I don't want to get all political, but there's a lot of Democrats up that way who need the Lord. If you think the Lord is nudging you to help, then talk to me after church."

His wife began to weep quietly. Four hundred balloons! she thought. He'll wear himself out. Lord, send him helpers.

It had been a rough couple months for Dale's wife. When the chickens died, effectively ending their Scripture eggs ministry, she felt God had let them down. She tried talking with Dale about it, but it only upset him.

"The ways of the Lord are not ours to understand," he told her. "I can only believe he has something finer in store for us."

Then to see Dale's faith rewarded with the salvation balloons ministry was such a joy.

There was a rustle by the organ. Bea Majors rose to her feet. "I'll help you blow up the balloons, Dale."

"Count me in, too," said Bill Muldock from the back row.

Dale's wife began weeping in earnest. I'm sorry for ever doubting you, Lord. Thank you, thank you, thank you.

Dale was still standing, sniffling. He pulled a handkerchief from his pocket. "Thank you, friends. I can't tell you what this means to me. The Lord bless you."

Sam Gardner was praying also. Dear God, please let him sit down now.

But Dale couldn't be stopped, not when the hand of the Lord was so clearly upon him. "I need your prayers for a rare north wind. Ladies, I know it might hurt your petunias, but with Dubois County straight south of us, I need a strong north wind to reach the Catholics in those parts."

Bea Majors frowned. She'd just planted two flats of pink petunias. She prayed, but not too hard.

Dale spent the next three days experimenting with his balloons. He discovered if he filled the balloons with less helium, the balloons would fall to the ground much sooner. He called it "target evangelism." On Wednesday evening, he released twenty balloons a mile upwind from a Kingdom Hall just as the Jehovah's Witnesses were gathering to worship. On Thursday, he floated another twenty balloons toward the Masonic Lodge in Cartersburg.

On Friday morning, when Dale was eating breakfast, their telephone rang. Dale picked it up and said hello.

"I'm looking for a Mr. Dale Hinshaw," a man said.

"You got him."

"I'm calling about one of your balloons."

Dale was faint with excitement. "Where are you?"

"I'm in Pittsburgh with the zoo. One of your balloons landed in our aviary exhibit, and our trumpeter swan choked on it and died. Do you know how many trumpeter swans there are in the world, Mr. Hinshaw?"

"Uh, no."

"One less than there used to be, thanks to you and your balloon."

Dale didn't know what to say. "You can take comfort knowing your swan's in a better place," he said finally.

It troubled Dale. He'd never meant to kill a swan. He liked swans. He and the missus had three concrete swans in their front yard. He thought about giving up his salvation balloons ministry, until it occurred to him that was just what the devil would want.

Satan's behind this for sure, he thought. He wants to stop my ministry. Well, he can forget about that. It's not gonna happen.

Bea Majors and Bill Muldock came the next morning. Dale and his wife wrote out the plan of salvation four hundred times on small slips of paper while Bill and Bea inflated the balloons and tied them on. They finished in late afternoon. Dale phoned Bob Miles at the *Herald*, who came with his camera.

Dale wet his finger and raised it in the air. "It's blowing from the southwest. That oughta carry 'em toward Lake Erie. Let's pray they'll hit a west wind up there and head toward New York City. Lots of perverts there. Let's pray the Lord'll blow his breath on these balloons and take them right into the Big Apple."

"Amen to that," said Bea.

"Bill, could you raise the garage door?"

"It'd be my honor." He raised the garage door and they pushed the balloons out, all four hundred at once. They rose in the air, a riot of color. Bob Miles snapped a picture.

"Glory hallelujah!" said Bea Majors. "It makes me want to play the organ."

Dale wiped away a tear. His wife reached over and took his hand. Even Bob Miles, a hardened journalist, was moved. "That's some ministry you got there, Dale. I'll be sure to write up a story about it."

Lord, don't let this go to my head, Dale prayed. Keep me humble, so all the glory can go to you.

They watched until the balloons were little dots in the northeast sky.

"It looks like they're headed toward Canada," Bill Muldock observed.

"I always wanted an international ministry," Dale said. His wife squeezed his hand.

Two blocks over, Sam Gardner sat on his front porch watching the balloons float away. He wasn't sure what to think of Dale's salvation balloons ministry. He was skeptical anytime someone boiled the wondrous mystery of salvation down to four simple points, but he didn't doubt Dale's sincerity. His sanity, yes, but not his sincerity. The funny thing was, Sam believed God could use the salvation balloons to reach someone. Sam preferred talking to people about God, but if Dale was more comfortable using balloons, Sam supposed God could use that, too.

Sam was trying hard not to be a theological snob. Maybe God did want Dale to do this. Maybe tomorrow, a man walking along the shores of Lake Erie, despondent that his wife had left him, would find a shriveled balloon lying on the sand, pick it up, pray a prayer, and be flooded with peace. Maybe next week a runaway teenager in a back alley in New York City would pick up a balloon, find hope, and turn toward home. Sam hoped so.

He thought maybe he'd talk about it in his sermon the next day. How we cast these gospel seeds out into the wind and trust God to help them grow into a radiant, glorious tree that gives shade and comfort to a weary world.

Seven

The Odd Fellows

It was the eighth of July, and Harvey Muldock was waxing his 1951 Plymouth Cranbrook convertible in preparation for the Fourth of July parade. The parade had been scheduled for the fourth, but Harvey and Eunice were out of town that weekend visiting Eunice's sister. Harvey has the only convertible in town and won't let anyone else drive it, so the town council moved the Fourth of July parade to the middle of the month so Harvey and his Plymouth could be there.

There was some grumbling about the Fourth of July parade being moved and a few anonymous letters to the editor. In defiance, the Shriners marched on the fourth anyway, but since Bernie, the policeman, didn't stop traffic, the Shriners ended up spread out over several blocks. It looked more like a rash of jaywalking than a parade.

Harvey has led the town parades — the

Fourth of July parade and the Corn and Sausage Days parade — since 1963, when he took the Cranbrook in on a trade. Before that, the high-school band led the parades, but when Harvey acquired the convertible, he was promoted to the head of the line. He'd gone nearly eighty parades without a mishap and thought he was pushing his luck. The pressure was getting to him. He'd been thinking of putting the Cranbrook up on blocks and retiring from the parade.

The Cranbrook has lately been a source of contention in the Muldock home. Harvey and Eunice have a one-car garage, which the Cranbrook has occupied since 1963. Eunice parks her car in the driveway underneath the oak tree where the birds powder their noses. It's a big tree. Harvey thinks it might be the largest tree in town. Eunice told him to either cut down the tree or let her park her car in the garage, out of range. She gave him forty years to get it done, and when he didn't, she moved her car to the garage and demoted the Cranbrook to the driveway.

Even though Harvey had been planning on retiring the Cranbrook, for Eunice to just kick it out of the garage, for her to so casually dismiss its many contributions, troubled Harvey.

"I don't know what's gotten into her," he

said at the Monday night meeting of the Odd Fellows. "Now she's telling me I oughta sell it. Says we don't have room for it. That car never did anything to her. I don't know what's gotten into her."

"Used to be a man's garage was his castle," Vinny Toricelli said. "Now women have even take that over. Next thing you know, they'll be wanting to join the lodge."

The Odd Fellows Lodge is in the basement of the *Herald* building. It's dark and mildewy and hasn't been cleaned in years. There's an old black-and-white TV in one corner. Above the TV is the Miss Lugwrench calendar, which they take down and hide whenever a member of the clergy visits. In the closet underneath the stairs is a rusty old toilet and a sink where they get the water for their coffee. No self-respecting woman would be caught dead in the place.

The Harmony chapter of the Odd Fellows was founded in 1929, when the first lodge members swore a sacred oath to "visit the sick, relieve the distressed, bury the dead, and educate the orphans," according to the engraved plaque next to the Miss Lugwrench calendar. Now they mostly sit around and watch ball games on the TV in the corner. They installed a phone in 1967, but when their wives started calling to track them down, they took it out. They like their privacy, the freedom to exercise their First Amendment rights in peace. They complain about their wives and how none of the younger men in town want to join their lodge. It worries them, to see the Odd Fellow legacy dwindle to an end. They think maybe a cookout would help generate interest.

"Yeah, we gotta do that someday," Harvey said. "We could do it at my house. Eunice wouldn't care. Yeah, we oughta do that this summer yet."

Asa Peacock said, "Maybe we could plan a trip of some sort. That might stir up some interest."

"Where do you think we could go?" Harvey asked.

Ellis Hodge suggested they charter a bus and tour the fish farm north of Martinsville.

Kyle Weathers, the town's barber, thought a trip to the barbershop museum in Connecticut might appeal to potential Odd Fellows.

Asa Peacock told of a story he'd read the day before in the *Hoosier Farmer* magazine. "This fella over near Ladoga took apart a 1953 Farmall tractor and rebuilt it in the loft of his barn. They had a picture of it and everything. Maybe we could go see that."

They discussed other ideas, but by then Harvey wasn't listening. His mind was fixed on that tractor in the hayloft.

The next morning, he ate breakfast, showered, and then went outside to measure the attic of his garage. Then he measured the Cranbrook. It would just fit. Even the antenna with the raccoon tail cleared the rafters. It was meant to be.

Harvey Muldock has never been a religious man. He's gone to church all his married life, mostly to keep Eunice from nagging at him. He had never understood it when people would stand and talk about God leading them to do something. But seeing everything come together, he knew a force bigger than him was at work.

It took Harvey a week to take apart the Cranbrook and reassemble it in the garage attic. He didn't do anything else the entire time, didn't go to work or church. He even skipped the next week's lodge meeting, which set the Odd Fellows to speculating. They thought maybe Harvey and the Cranbrook had left town.

"Can't say as I blame him," Vinny Toricelli said. "A man can take only so much, after all."

They complained for a while about the decline of the American family. Vinny told of hearing the Reverend Johnny LaCosta talk on TV about how the liberal Supreme Court had emasculated America's manhood and how it was time for Christian men to stand up and be counted and assert themselves as the head of the family.

"Ain't he the guy who's always talking against the Catholics?" Asa Peacock asked. "I thought you were Catholic."

"This is bigger than any one religion," Vinny said. "This is about our country. This is about America's manhood."

Meanwhile, back at the Muldocks', Harvey's manhood was exhausted. Carrying a car up a ladder was hard work, even if you did it in pieces. He took a shower, went to bed, and fell asleep almost immediately.

Around six in the morning, just as the sun was coming up, Harvey heard a crash. He thought it was a burglar trying to kick in their back door, until he remembered they never locked it. He got out of bed, put on his bathrobe, and went downstairs to look around. Everything was fine. He went outside and walked around the house.

Walking past the garage, he noticed the roof was sagging. He swung open the garage doors, and there was the Cranbrook, balanced neatly on top of Eunice's car. Remarkably, the Cranbrook was hardly scratched. Eunice's car, apart from the top two feet, was in pretty good shape, too. If you slouched down in the seat, you could probably still drive it.

Harvey was trying to figure out the best way to tell Eunice when she appeared at his side. To her credit, she didn't say much. The benefit of being married to a car dealer is that when he crushes your car, he can get you a new one. She just looked at the Cranbrook perched on top of her car, shook her head, and said, "Would you like some coffee?" Yes, he thought he would. They went inside, sat at the kitchen table, and drank their coffee.

"I suppose maybe I should have thought about reinforcing the attic floor," Harvey admitted over his second cup of coffee. "It's the heaviest car Plymouth made in 1951. Three thousand, three hundred pounds."

"Probably that would have been a good idea," Eunice said. She wanted to say more, but she didn't. She drank more coffee to keep from saying anything. She was already on her fifth cup.

Harvey took a shower, got dressed, and went out to the garage to start Eunice's car. There wasn't much headroom. He had to lie down across the front seat to fit in, but it did start. He eased the gearshift down one notch to reverse, but the cars, stacked one atop the other, wouldn't clear the garage door. He turned off the engine and began reflecting on the situation, still lying down across the front seat.

Charlie Gardner, watching from his front porch across the street, walked over to observe the proceedings. This was a scenario Harvey had hoped to avoid.

Charlie was trying hard not to laugh, as if two cars stacked one atop the other was an everyday occurrence.

"I'm no expert at these kinds of things, never having had this happen to me," he said, "but I've heard that people in similar situations have let the air out of the tires on the bottom car. You might try that. It might buy you four or five inches."

Harvey hadn't thought of that. It might just work. He let the air out of the tires, and the cars just cleared the door. Now, instead of the cars being hidden in the garage, they were in plain view of everyone driving past. Before long, a small crowd had gathered. They all had suggestions, most of them dumb. Dale Hinshaw thought they could tie helium balloons to the Cranbrook and float it off Eunice's car.

For the next two days Harvey sat in his lawn chair under the oak tree looking at the cars and reflecting. On Thursday night, he telephoned the Odd Fellows, all fifty-three of them, and invited them to his house the next evening for a cookout. They all came, mostly to look at the cars.

Harvey fed them beans and wienies. After they ate, he looped four stout ropes under the Cranbrook, climbed a ladder leaning against the oak tree, and pulled the ropes over two thick branches situated just above the car. "Okay, men, all of you now, grab a rope and, on the count of three, pull."

"Are you crazy?" Kyle Weathers said. "We can't lift that car. You're crazy."

"Thirty-three hundred pounds divided by fifty-three men equals sixty-two pounds apiece. It's not that heavy if we all pull together. But if you don't think you can do it, if you're not strong enough, you don't have to help."

Suddenly, lifting the Cranbrook was a test of manhood. The Supreme Court might have tried to emasculate America's manhood, but they had not succeeded in the Harmony chapter of the Odd Fellows Lodge.

They rose from their lawn chairs. Yes, they could do it. Sixty-two pounds was a lark, a walk in the park for an Odd Fellow, who, after all, had taken a sacred oath to relieve the distressed, and Harvey was distressed, was he not?

They spit on their hands and grabbed the ropes.

"Pull!" Harvey cried. The Odd Fellows pulled on the ropes, and the Cranbrook rose in the air, tentatively at first, but then confidently and with purpose.

"Hold her steady, men," Harvey shouted. He leaped in Eunice's car, lay across the seat, fired up the engine, slid the gearshift down one notch, and backed it out from underneath the Cranbrook.

"Now ease her down," he cried out. "Gentle, gentle."

They lowered the Cranbrook to the ground, unblemished. Oh, they were proud. Fifty-three Odd Fellows celebrating their manhood and upholding their pledge to relieve the distressed. They walked around the Cranbrook, admiring it and patting each other on the back.

"Too bad Bob Miles wasn't here to take a picture for the *Herald*," Asa Peacock said.

"I could go fetch him," said Ellis Hodge. He climbed in his truck and returned ten minutes later with Bob and his camera. They hoisted the Cranbrook into the air while Bob snapped a picture; then they lowered it to the ground.

They raised and lowered the car five more times that night, as word got out and people came past to behold this miracle of physics. Some of the younger men who came by wanted to lift the car, but the Odd Fellows wouldn't let them. "Members only," they said. "Of course, if you want to join, we'd be happy to have you." They signed up a dozen new members that night alone. One dozen strapping young men lined up in Harvey's driveway pledging to visit the sick, relieve the distressed, bury the dead, and educate the orphans. It brought tears to Harvey's eyes.

The next morning dawned bright and sunny. Harvey waxed the Cranbrook, then drove it to the school where they were assembling for the Fourth of July parade. Harvey took his place at the head of the line. It wasn't about what he wanted, he knew that now. It was about duty, about destiny. The Cranbrook didn't belong locked away in a garage for only Harvey to enjoy. There were parades to lead and the distressed in need of relief. If he didn't do it, who would?

He patted the Cranbrook on the dashboard. "You're looking good, old girl."

Bernie, the policeman, blew his whistle. Harvey moved the gearshift down three notches and eased forward. He didn't even have to steer. After eighty parades, the

Cranbrook knew the way. Harvey sat behind the wheel, waving to the crowds. Someday, he knew, he'd have to pass on the glory to someone else. But today was not that day.

Eight
True Riches

It's been two years since Ellis and Miriam adopted Amanda from Ellis's no-good brother, Ralph. They had to pay Ralph thirty thousand dollars, all the money they had in the world. At the time it seemed like the right thing to do, but ever since Ellis has worried about going broke. He's had to borrow money to run the farm and thinks he might have to sell it off, move into town, and get a job at the glove factory in Cartersburg.

Amanda is fourteen now and poised to enter the eighth grade. In the sixth grade, she won the National Spelling Bee and shook the president's hand. She's the closest thing Harmony ever had to a celebrity, and in a fit of excitement they made her the Lifetime Honorary Grand Marshall of the Corn and Sausage Days parade and erected a sign at the town limits: *Welcome to Harmony! The Home of Amanda Hodge! Winner of the*

Natunal Spelling Bee! Ervin Matthews painted the sign, but misspelled the word *national,* a sad irony for a sign honoring the winner of a spelling bee. The next winter, the sign was knocked over by a snowplow and, preferring to leave well enough alone, no one bothered to put it back.

Meanwhile, Amanda has moved on to other triumphs. This past winter, she was invited to join the Future Problem Solvers of America, which involved a five-day trip to Atlanta over spring break for the Future Problem Solvers of America's annual convention. Although Ellis was proud of her, he was weary of shelling out travel money. When he was a kid, he belonged to the 4-H, which involved a visit to Charlie Barker's Angus farm and a bus trip to the state fair. They packed their lunches, ate on the bus, and were home in time to milk cows that evening.

He asked Amanda what kind of problems she was supposed to solve in Atlanta.

"Oh, global warming and overpopulation and things like that," she said.

He let out a little snort. He tried not to snort around Amanda, but sometimes it couldn't be helped.

"What is it with the schools these days?" he complained to Miriam. "Why are they sending her all the way to Atlanta to solve problems? There's lots of problems around here that need solving, if you ask me. Like how I'm gonna pay for her to go to Atlanta. Why can't she just join a softball team and stay home."

That was in late March and Ellis is still snorting. Whenever he hears about global warming, he says to Miriam, "Humph, I thought we solved that problem back in Atlanta."

The money's always been tight, but with Amanda it's even worse. Twenty dollars here, fifty dollars there. The tractor's been broke for a month, and they don't have the money to get it fixed. Then, to top it off, Pastor Sam stopped past one evening and asked if they needed help from the church. Ellis tried to laugh it off, but he was embarrassed. "No, thank you, Sam. You give that money to someone who needs it. We're doing just fine."

When Sam left, Ellis stalked around the house, grouching about how the church people were talking about them and vowing not to go on church welfare. He glared at Miriam. "How did they know we were having problems? You must have said something at the Friendly Women's Circle. What did you tell them?"

"I've not said a word to anyone. And I don't appreciate your tone of voice."

Then they began picking at one another and over the next few days began commenting on matters they used to let slide.

"Do you have to scrape your fork against the plate like that?" Ellis asked Miriam one evening during supper. "It's rather irritating."

"I wish you wouldn't clip your toenails in the bathroom and just leave them on the floor," Miriam told Ellis the next day. "Would it kill you to sweep them up?"

In June, Amanda was invited to join the Debutante Club at Opal Majors's house. Opal takes in farm girls and teaches them which fork to use, how to sit like a lady, and how to walk with books on their heads. After a month of lessons, they rent a limousine and travel to the city for dinner at the revolving restaurant on top of the insurance building and an opera. The program runs a hundred dollars — limousine, dinner, and opera not included.

Amanda couldn't decide whether to join the Debutante Club or the softball team, which costs twenty dollars and culminates in a trip to Cartersburg for the county tourney and a hot dog and chips from the concession stand.

Ellis pushed her toward the softball program.

He gave her the mitt he'd used as a kid, but after forty years the leather had rotted and it was falling apart. Miriam thought Amanda should have a mitt of her own, so over Ellis's objections they drove her into town to Uly Grant's hardware store to scrutinize the mitts for sale. There were two mitts in stock — a left handed first-baseman's mitt, which Uly's father ordered by mistake in the late sixties, and a brand-new genuine cowhide mitt marked seventy-five dollars, which was seventy-five more dollars than Ellis had counted on spending.

The first-baseman's mitt was eighteen dollars. Ellis tried to steer Amanda toward it by pointing out how useful it would be if she could throw with either hand, but Miriam glared at him, so Ellis had to dip into the emergency hundred-dollar bill he kept hidden in his wallet. He wasn't happy about it and complained the whole way home until Amanda was practically in tears. She told Ellis she'd get a job and pay him back the money.

Miriam had been taught by her parents that husbands and wives should never go to bed mad. But if she had abided by that, she'd have stayed awake the entire month of

June. She was that mad at Ellis. She didn't speak to him for several weeks, except for the essentials, and only then with a poisoned courtesy.

In late June, Ellis relocated to the barn to live with the cows. He moved his recliner out there, along with a television set and a box fan. He ventured into the house just long enough to eat. After a while, he began to smell like the cows, which, if you're residing with cows, you tend not to notice. But Miriam did, and said she wouldn't be offended if he ate his meals out in the barn, too.

"Fine with me," Ellis mumbled under his breath. "At least the cows don't argue."

The downside of never fighting is that you've never learned how to make up, so Miriam and Ellis were locked in a stalemate. Living in the barn seemed easier than resolving their differences, so Ellis stayed put. He even stopped going to church, except for the Furnace Committee meeting.

Miriam would stand at the sink of an evening washing the dishes and looking out the window toward the barn. Every now and then, she'd catch Ellis watching back. It went on like that, Ellis in the barn and Miriam in the house, until one evening in late July, when Miriam found Amanda crying in her bedroom about how everything was her fault and how Miriam and Ellis would have been better off never to have adopted her. She wanted to take the mitt back to the store. She hadn't used it much. Maybe they could get their money back, she told Miriam.

"It's not your fault, honey. Things like this happen sometimes. It'll work out. Don't worry."

Miriam sat with Amanda until she fell asleep, then went downstairs and sat in her chair. There was an empty spot where Ellis's chair had been. She began to cry. All these years they'd been married with never a hard word, and now this. Foolish pride, that's all it was. She went out to the barn and there he was, sitting in his recliner, dejected.

"I miss you," she said.

He sniffed. His stubbly chin trembled. "I miss you, too."

"Would you come back home?"

"If you'll have me," he said.

They carried his chair into the house. It smelled like the cows. Miriam was going to say something, then decided against it. Instead, she ran a tub of water and they took a bath together, like they did when they were first married and were thinner and could fit in a bathtub together. Now it was a tighter fit, but they didn't mind. They bathed one another. Miriam had to go over Ellis twice to get the cow smell off. Then they went to bed and held each other and made their peace, this anxious farmer who worried about money and his wife, who didn't always understand him, but loved him anyway.

When they woke up the next morning, Amanda was gone. Her bed was made and her baseball mitt was on the pillow along with a note saying how sorry she was to cause so much trouble. Inside the mitt were thirty dollars and an IOU to Ellis for forty-five dollars. Her bicycle was gone from the back porch, along with her backpack.

They called Bernie, the policeman, then got in their truck and drove the roads between their house and town, looking in the ditches, sick with fear. They barely spoke, except for every now and then Ellis would choke up and say it was all his fault for being so cheap.

A little before noon, they found her bike behind the Rexall drugstore in town, where she'd bought a bus ticket to the city. Bernie phoned ahead to the police. Then Miriam and Ellis got in his car, and they drove to the city to find her. Bernie ran his siren the whole way there, weaving in and out of the traffic, with Ellis and Miriam clutching one another in the backseat, wishing they'd followed in their truck.

Bernie has been the policeman in Harmony ever since his brother-in-law, Harvey Muldock, was on the town board and they needed a policeman. He's kept the job because it's a small town, he's a nice guy, and letting him go would cause hard feelings. But he's not real smart. He told Ellis and Miriam not to worry, that if they didn't find Amanda, they could always put her picture on a milk carton.

"Look on the bright side," he said. "Maybe they'll mention on the milk carton that she was the National Spelling Bee champion. That would make a nice keepsake."

The police in the city nabbed Amanda as she was coming off the bus. They took her to the police station until Miriam and Ellis arrived with Bernie. The police made them talk with a social worker, which embarrassed Ellis. They took Amanda off by herself in a room and asked her questions about Ellis. He felt like a criminal. Then they let Miriam and Ellis visit with Amanda alone. Ellis apologized about the mitt.

"Amanda, honey, you don't know this yet, but when you're an adult, you worry about things like money. I've just been anxious, that's all. I sure didn't aim to take it out on you."

She told him not to worry, that one day she'd invent something and make them all rich.

Ellis chuckled at that. "If anyone could, honey, it'd be you. You're the smartest kid around."

Finally, late in the afternoon, they let them go home.

Bernie dropped them off at the Rexall, where they'd left their truck. It was supper time. They hadn't eaten all day.

"It's Italian Night at the Coffee Cup," Ellis said. "What say we grab a bite to eat?"

"Can we afford it?" Miriam asked.

Ellis grinned and rubbed Amanda's head. "Why, sure we can. We're rich. We've got Amanda, after all. She's our treasure."

They ate from the buffet, while Bea Majors played Italian tunes on the organ. She knew only five songs, but they sat through three cycles, drinking in the atmosphere. Ellis reached over and took Miriam's hand. "What a life we have," he marveled. "Aren't we blessed!" He kissed the top of Amanda's head. "How's our treasure? Did you get enough to eat?"

It was just like the old days.

The next Saturday, they drove to Cartersburg for the county softball tourney. It was a beautiful summer day. The temperature was in the high seventies; there were just enough puffy clouds to cast shade. Amanda's team lost twenty-three to nothing, which everyone took in stride, having lost all their games this season. At first they would get all worked up and yell and scream, but failing so spectacularly has eased the pressure. Now the parents relax and visit while their children are mauled; then they eat a hot dog and chips and watch the next game.

Amanda was secretly pleased her team lost. When she first came to live with Ellis and Miriam, she feared the only reason they wanted her was because she'd won the National Spelling Bee. She worried what would happen if she lost at something, whether they would still love her. So to lose all the games and still have Ellis and Miriam rub her head and tell her they were proud of her and not to be discouraged because there was always next year was a consolation to her.

She still didn't understand why Ellis had lived in the barn for a month. They hadn't discussed such things at the Future Problem Solvers of America's annual convention. They'd stuck to the easy stuff like overpopulation and global warming. Someone else was going to have to figure out Ellis. Someone a lot smarter than she was.

As for Ellis, he ate his hot dog and watched the game and thought back to when he was little and life was simple. Although he has this vague memory that maybe it wasn't easy for everyone. He remembers his mother standing at the kitchen sink, looking out the window toward the barn where his father was, not speaking, a tear running down her cheek. Maybe that's what it meant to be an adult. To weep for reasons children didn't understand. He wasn't sure. Someone else was going to have to figure that out. Someone a lot smarter than he was.

Nine

The Amazing Whipples

Ever since their kids were little, the Dale Hinshaws have taken off the first week of July to go fishing up north. Except this year. With their salvation balloons ministry just getting off the ground, they'd skipped their vacation in order to serve the Lord. In the past month, they'd released two thousand salvation balloons. As a result, a family of five from Wisconsin had come to the Lord, and there had been only one casualty — the death by suffocation of a farsighted trumpeter swan who'd mistaken a withered balloon for a plant shoot, to its eternal regret.

Dale had aimed the salvation balloons toward Chicago in hopes of bringing a few Democrats to the Lord. The wind had pushed one balloon north to Fond du Lac, where it was found by the father of the Amazing Whipples, a family of tumblers, who were performing for the summer at the Lake Winnebago Amusement Park and

Petting Zoo. The Amazing Whipple parents had three daughters, each of whom had blossomed into feminine fullness, which was evident when they wore their tight leotards.

In early August, Dale received a letter from the Amazing Whipple father thanking him for flying the salvation balloon their way. Because of Dale, all the family had repented, were thinking of changing their name to the Amazing Grace Whipples, and were now tumbling for the Lord. They enclosed a picture of the shapely Amazing Whipple daughters arranged in the shape of a cross.

A week later, the phone rang at the Dale Hinshaw home. It was the Amazing Whipple father. The Lord had told him not to let his daughters perform in leotards anymore, that it inflamed worldly desires in the hearts of men, so he had them tumble in sweatpants instead. Attendance had declined precipitously, and the park manager was letting them go.

They were discouraged. Their only desire had been to tumble for the Lord. Now they'd been fired and were low on money. They believed God was leading them to bring their tumbling ministry to churches. But they needed funding. Could Dale help?

They would pay him back, he promised. The Amazing Whipple father began to weep over the phone.

He talked about their life before they'd met the Lord, how they'd compromised their morals to make money and done things they weren't proud of, things he'd rather not talk about, things they might have to do again if no one helped them. They hadn't realized being Christian was such a burden. They were weakening in their faith. Could Dale help them?

Dale asked how much money they needed.

The father wasn't sure, but thought a thousand dollars would see them through. Their van needed work, and the girls needed matching sweatpants.

"I know it sounds silly," he told Dale, "but if we wore matching costumes when we tumbled for Satan, we need to look even nicer when we tumble for the Lord."

Dale couldn't argue with that.

He went to the bank, cashed in a CD, drove over to Cartersburg to the Western Union, and wired the Amazing Whipples a thousand dollars. It was a lot of money, but he felt responsible, since it had been his salvation balloon that had caused them to lose their job. If it hadn't been for that, the Whipple daughters would still be gainfully employed in their leotards, inflaming worldly desires in the hearts of men.

The father had promised to call when the money came, so Dale hung close to the phone. But it didn't ring that day or the next. Dale called the Western Union and asked if the money had gone through. He could hear the operator pecking away on her computer. "Yes, sir, our records indicate the money was picked up."

On the third day, Dale phoned directory assistance and asked for the number of the Amazing Whipples from Fond du Lac, Wisconsin.

The operator told him there were no Whipples in Fond du Lac. "But I do have a listing for an Ingrid and her Amazing Whip."

"That may be it," Dale said. "What's the number?"

He copied the number down, then phoned. It rang five times, before a machine came on. "This is Ingrid. I'm not here, but you can leave a message." Her voice sounded slurred, as if she'd been drinking. There was whooping in the background and rock music.

Oh, Lord, I'm too late, Dale thought. He left his name and number on the machine. It made him uneasy. He worried that the Amazing Whipples had stumbled in the faith and were back to wearing leotards. He fretted for two days, before speaking to the missus. "I got a feeling something ain't right. I think we oughta get in the car and go up there and see if we can find 'em. I know it's crazy, but I think they need us."

They packed that morning, then called Sam Gardner to come by once a day and feed their cat. At the bottom of Sam's contract, in small print, it reads, "Pastor will also be responsible for ministering to members as the Lord might lead." He ends up making a lot of airport runs and feeding pets and mowing yards while people are on vacation. During his annual review, they evaluate whether or not he has a servant's heart and adjust his pay accordingly.

It was Sam's fault. When he was being interviewed, he'd insisted on a written contract to keep from getting fired in the middle of the year. They'd balked at first, but then had given in and proceeded to fill the contract with vague requirements that could be interpreted to mean anything they wanted, up to and including lawn maintenance and pet care.

The contract was eight pages long, typed, single-spaced. Any annoying thing any pastor had ever done was expressly forbidden, and these people had long memories, recalling aggravations from decades before. It stipulated how Sam should dress, where he should live, and how if someone in the church died while he was on vacation, he was to come home. It listed a myriad of rules dictating his every move. Then, fearing they might have left something out, they added, "Pastor will also be responsible for ministering to members as the Lord might lead."

Sam had suggested the contract talk about their partnership in the work of the Lord, but Fern Hampton had shot that down at their first meeting. "If we're partners, then how come you're the only one getting paid. I say if we're going to be partners, we should all get paid. What's good for the goose is good for the gander, that's what I say."

By the time they were done drafting the contract, Sam's pay had been cut two thousand dollars and he'd lost his education expense account.

"The problem today is that too many ministers got too much education as it is," Dale Hinshaw had said. "Whatever happened to a good, old-fashioned, simple faith? Maybe if these pastors would pray a little more instead of burying their heads in books, we'd all be better off." And that was the demise of Sam's education expense account.

Then Fern Hampton tried to sink his transportation expense account by pointing out that he lived within walking distance of the meetinghouse, and why should the church pay for his gas when the walk would do him good? "And as long as we're making out a contract, I don't understand why we're paying for his health insurance. It seems to me if he had a little more faith, he'd trust the Lord to heal him when he got sick."

Dale Hinshaw said, "Speaking of trusting the Lord, maybe we need to ask Sam whether he even believes in the Lord. I mean, why should we even be paying a minister who may not believe in God? It's putting the cart before the horse, if you ask me."

No one had asked him, though that had never stopped Dale from offering his opinion.

That was two years ago and now the contract was largely forgotten, except when someone needed Sam to watch their pets, which is how he found himself at Dale's house the next day, opening a can of 9 Lives and spooning it into a bowl.

He was washing the spoon when the phone rang. It rang six times before he heard the answering machine click on in the living room. He walked in to listen. He heard the whir of tape, then a woman's voice. "Yeah, this is Ingrid. I'm calling for Dale. He called about my whip act, I suppose. I charge five hundred dollars for a personal appearance, and if the cops bust us, you have to pay the fines."

Sam was disgusted, but not surprised. It was always the finger-pointers who had the secrets. For as long as Sam could remember, Dale had railed against anyone with the nerve to disagree with him on a matter of faith. Now his dirty secret was out, and Sam had proof.

He opened the answering machine, took out the cassette tape and put it in his pocket. It really wasn't stealing, he told himself. It was more a seizure of evidence. Besides, Sam had a congregation to protect. It said so in his contract, on the fifth page. "Pastor will be responsible for the spiritual well-being of the church members."

He had argued against it at the time. "How can I be responsible for your spiritual well-being? Isn't that up to you?"

Fern Hampton had cocked her head and stared at him. "Now, Sam, if we wanted to be responsible for our own spiritual well-being, why would we hire a minister? That's what we pay you to do. It concerns me that you're shirking your duties before you've even begun. Are you sure the Lord has called you to be a minister? I don't see much evidence of spiritual maturity on your part."

Miriam Hodge had come to his defense. "How we can ask Sam to be in charge of our spiritual well-being? Although he might have an influence on our spiritual growth, aren't we finally responsible for our own faith?"

That led to a three-hour discussion on whether the pastor should be held accountable for the spiritual health of the church members.

"The way I see it," Dale Hinshaw had said, "is that if I commit a sin, but I don't know it's a sin because Sam never preached against it, then Sam should be the one who goes to hell, not me."

Everyone but Sam and Miriam had sided with Dale, which resulted in a line in the contract requiring Sam to post on the bulletin board a list of sins people shouldn't commit.

The good thing is that these people are rather conventional sinners with limited imaginations. It didn't take Sam long to come up with a list of sins they might commit. Gossip, thoughts of lust, some cheating on taxes, a few fishing lies, and an occasional dalliance with Unitarianism while on vacation. Once, after Johnny Mackey's car went missing, it appeared one of them was a car thief. But it turned out Johnny had loaned it to Ellis Hodge, and it had slipped his mind.

But Dale Hinshaw consorting with Ingrid and her amazing whip was real sin. At the very least it was lust, maybe even adultery, both of which were listed on the bulletin board. Honest-to-goodness, genuine, old-fashioned sin. And Sam had him dead to rights. On tape!

He wasn't quite sure how to go about it, whether he should confront Dale gently, as advised by 2 Timothy 2:25, or come right out and smite him according to the book of Leviticus. By the time the Dale Hinshaws returned on Saturday, Sam had decided to preach a sermon against adultery, in hopes Dale might come to his senses, stop fraternizing with Ingrid and her amazing whip, and return to his wife of forty-one years with her sensible shoes and support hose.

When they came into meeting that Sunday, Sam pulled Dolores Hinshaw aside for a private moment and asked how she was doing. She sniffed and dabbed her eyes. "There's some people who say they're Christians, but they aren't. You trust them, but they let you down." She sniffed again.

Sam gave her a hug. "You needn't say anything more. I know exactly what you mean."

He was livid to see the pain Dale had caused this fine woman. Sam had never been one to preach on sin, preferring to focus on more positive matters, such as love and forgiveness and everyone working together at the annual Chicken Noodle Dinner. But this was not a time for soft talk. This was a time for admonishment and rebuke.

People were settling in for their customary naps, when Sam stood and began reading from the book of Leviticus, warning of death to adulterers; every now and then he raised his head to look at Dale, who appeared unconcerned over the pain he'd caused. By now, people were wide awake and wondering where Sam was headed.

It was then Sam moved in for the coup de grâce, the stroke of mercy. He closed his Bible and pointed in the general direction of Dale. He softened his voice. "But even for the adulterer, there can be forgiveness, if he but humbly confesses his sin and seeks God's pardon." With that assurance, Sam sat down in the Quaker silence, waiting for Dale to come forward and throw himself on the mercy of the Lord. It would be a beautiful moment. Sam would lay his hand on Dale's foul, sinful flesh and announce forgiveness, and maybe even return the tape.

After several minutes, Sam looked up. Everyone was staring at him, wondering with whom he had committed adultery and when. He'd gone to a pastor's conference the month before, or so he'd claimed. It must have been then. Now, consumed with guilt, he was ready to come clean. They weren't surprised. It was always the finger-pointers who had the secrets.

Fern Hampton was trying to recall which page of Sam's contract forbade adultery. She knew it was in there. She had insisted on it. There was something about Sam, a smoothness about him she'd never trusted. She had told Opal Majors, "It's the ones who preach about love that you got to keep an eye on. Next thing you know, they're out hugging everyone, and you know what happens then. Give me a hellfire preacher any day of the week, that's what I say."

Meanwhile, Sam sat behind the pulpit, waiting for Dale to say something. He wondered why he was taking so long, then worried that maybe he'd pressed him too hard. After all, despite what his contract says, you can't be responsible for someone else's spiritual well-being. Folks have to work out their own salvation. It was the Spirit's job to convict Dale of his sin, not his. Sam had his own problems, his own sins to confess. Like the theft of Dale's answering machine tape. He could feel the tape in his pants pocket. Maybe he shouldn't have taken it. He felt guilty.

Lord, why did I steal that tape? he said to himself. What was I thinking? As is often the case, Sam had become what he most despised — a finger-pointer.

People were still watching him. "I've done something terribly wrong," he said, in a quiet voice. He struggled to go on. "I can't go into any details." A few disappointed groans were heard. They'd been looking forward to the details. "But I ask God's forgiveness and your forgiveness also."

No one spoke for the longest time. Finally, Miriam Hodge stood, went to Sam, hugged him, and said he was forgiven, which Fern Hampton thought was a bit hasty, but she kept quiet.

Sam was faint with gratitude. It was so wonderful to have friends you could trust with your sin, people who wouldn't assume the worst about you, people who would forgive you even before you asked. Besides, maybe Dale had a good reason to talk with Ingrid and her amazing whip. Maybe he was trying to lead her to the Lord. Maybe she had found one of his salvation balloons and was calling to talk about the Lord. Sam hadn't thought of that.

Oh, Lord, forgive me for assuming the worst about him, he prayed. Forgive my self-righteous, judgmental spirit. He thought about that. He wasn't sure self-righteousness was on the list of sins he'd posted on the bulletin board. It if wasn't, he'd have to add it. Self-righteousness could do a lot of harm, after all. It's better to forgive and show mercy. Isn't that what he'd always preached?

They closed with a song. Then Sam stood at the back, hugging everyone as they passed. Some of them seemed a little hesitant, but that was to be expected. It would take time to forgive him for what he had done. Sam didn't hold that against them. Instead, he preferred to think the very best of them, just as they had done for him.

Ten

Vacation

With the crisis of Dale Hinshaw and Ingrid and her amazing whip behind him and the opening of school two weeks away, Sam Gardner thought it was maybe time to take the family on a little vacation. It was like this every year, Sam waiting until the last minute, when the popular vacation destinations were fully booked, then loading his family into the car to visit some obscure place. Just once, Barbara wanted to take a vacation they'd actually planned, instead of waiting for the vacation mood to hit Sam, then loading up the car, and lurching off in the direction of his latest interest.

Two years before, they'd taken the "highest points" vacation, when they'd driven to the highest point in each surrounding state. Last year, they'd taken the "hardware store" vacation, during which they'd visited small-town hardware stores in the southern half of the state. Sam had talked

146

of little else since and hinted that maybe this year they could visit the small-town hardware stores in the northern half of the state.

Barbara was less than enthusiastic. "If you think I'm going to spend another vacation hanging around hardware stores, you're crazy. Just once, I'd like a normal vacation, like other people."

The next Sunday, Ellis Hodge gave Sam an article he'd clipped from the *Hoosier Farmer* about round barns, which he read to Barbara and the boys at the supper table the Wednesday before their vacation.

"It says here there used to be twenty-three round barns in the state. Now there's only fourteen. You know, maybe we oughta go see them before they're all gone. Wouldn't that be fun? It'd sure give the boys something to tell their friends about."

Barbara tries to sound positive whenever the children are present, though it's getting increasingly difficult. "That's certainly a shame about those barns. Why don't we go see one or two, then maybe head up to Chicago and spend a few days at a hotel? I've always wanted to take the boys to the Museum of Science and Industry. I've heard it's really neat. Then we could see the rest of the barns next summer."

Sam frowned. "I don't know. These barns

147

might not last another year. I say we visit them this year, then save our money and go to Chicago next summer. Yeah, I think that's what we'll do."

Sam is getting more like his father every year, which Barbara knew would happen, but it's not making it any easier to take. When they were first married, he was careful to solicit her opinion. Now he just tells her what they're going to do and expects her to smile and go along. Some days, it's all she can do not to smack him.

She wonders if it's a pastor thing, if those verses in the Bible about the man being the head of the household haven't finally gotten to him. He's been quoting Scripture to her. They'll be arguing and he'll quote a passage from Romans, as if that settles everything. She's been reading the Bible, too, so she can quote back, but not many of the verses take the woman's side.

She was talking about it with Mabel Morrison. "That's religion for you," Mabel said. "The men start them up, slant things their way, then tell us God wants it that way. Then, if a woman rebels, they call her a sinner. Isn't that convenient?"

Mabel bought an ad in the *Harmony Herald* inviting freethinking women to meet at her house to reflect on the motherhood of

God. It caused a flood of letters to the editor prophesying Mabel's eternal damnation.

Back in June, she showed up at Harmony Friends Meeting thinking she'd give organized religion one more try. She attends the Live Free or Die Sunday school class, which was begun in 1960 by Robert J. Miles, Sr., but is now being taught by Dale Hinshaw, whom she enjoys tormenting. "Dale, when you say we have to follow every word in the Bible, do you also mean Leviticus 19:19, where it says not to wear a garment made of two kinds of material? The reason I'm asking is because that shirt you're wearing looks like a cotton-polyester blend to me, Dale. What have you got to say for yourself?"

Dale suggested at the next elders meeting that things around the church were getting lax, authority-wise, and maybe it was time for a little correction and reproof, starting with Mabel. But the rest of the elders didn't want to take her on and told Dale if he felt led to correct and reprove Mabel, he was on his own.

Barbara decided if Mabel could buck two thousand years of Christian tradition, she could stand up to Sam. She told him if he wanted to take a statewide tour of round barns, he could, but she and the boys were going to Chicago.

This feminist uprising has caused much grumbling at the Coffee Cup Restaurant, where the men gather each morning to philosophize, drink their coffee, and lament their difficult lives. They wonder why their wives can't be more like Heather Darnell, the waitress, who smiles and pours their coffee and asks if there is anything they need, anything at all.

The men advised Sam to take a stand, that if he caved in now Barbara would lead him around by the nose the rest of his life.

"Don't it say in the Bible somewhere that the man's in charge?" Vinny Toricelli asked Sam. "Or don't you Quakers follow the Bible anymore? Say what you will about us Catholics, at least our women know their place."

Vinny has been encouraging Dale Hinshaw to leave the Quakers and join up with the Catholics. That would be quite a coup, converting a Quaker to the "one, true church," even if it is Dale Hinshaw. When Quakers get upset, they join the Baptist church. Unless they have a little money; then they hook up with the Methodists. But no Quaker in Harmony has ever left to become a Catholic.

The only thing holding Dale back is the Catholics calling their priests "Father," which is expressly forbidden in Matthew

23:9. "Call no man your father on earth, for you have one Father, who is in heaven." Other than that, Dale thinks the Catholics have pretty well hit the nail on the head.

Vinny has been praying for the pope to hold fast and not cave in to the latest theological fads just to keep the women happy. "There's a reason we hire our popes from the old country," he told Dale. "The men over there, they don't take no guff from their women. You get an American pope in, and he'd be starting some committee to maybe talk about having women priests, and next thing you know, they'll be saying Mary wasn't a virgin. You watch and see."

To Sam's horror, he occasionally finds himself agreeing with Vinny and Dale. One morning at the Coffee Cup, he heard himself say, "You got that right." Quaker ministers were supposed to be progressive. They were supposed to champion equality, defend the oppressed, and generally annoy men like Dale and Vinny. Now here he was agreeing with them, which was further proof he needed a vacation, and that his wife might have a point.

He sat at the counter of the Coffee Cup thinking about vacation and listening to the men complaining. He didn't want to be like them. Maybe they should go to Chicago after all. Barbara asked for so little. She worked hard to keep up the house and take care of the boys. Then she asked for one little thing, to go to Chicago for vacation, and he'd said no. He was ashamed. He paid his bill, and then went home to his beloved wife, his equal, his partner in life. He found her in the basement, switching clothes to the dryer.

She looked up at him. He smiled, "Uh, say, I've been thinking about vacation. I don't really want to see those barns. I think we should go to Chicago. You're right. It'd be a good experience for the boys."

"No," she said, "I think you were right about the barns. They may not be here next year. Besides, you work hard and it's really your vacation, so let's do what you want. I'm sorry I lost my temper."

They went back and forth for an hour, Sam arguing for Chicago and Barbara pushing for the barns. The longer they argued, the more headstrong they became.

Finally Sam said, "You know what really bothers me. I'm trying to work with you here, but you always have to have your way. I don't remember my parents ever arguing like this. My dad just told us the way it was going to be, and that was it. Boy, do I wish things were still that way."

He knew it was the wrong thing to say as

soon as he said it. Barbara got real quiet and started to tremble, then said in a cold, low voice, "If you think I'm going to cave in just because your mother did, you better think again. I told you we could go see the barns, and that's what we're going to do."

The rest of the day was very quiet.

Sam went to the Coffee Cup the next morning. Vinny poured him a cup of coffee.

"So'd you set her straight?" he asked Sam. "You going to see the barns?"

"Yep, it looks that way."

"That's telling her. Good for you, Sam. That's a way to stick to your guns."

The other men congratulated him for standing up to tyranny, asserting his manhood, and quelling the feminist uprising.

"How'd you do it?" Vinny asked. "Did you just walk in there and tell her the way it was gonna be?"

"Something like that," Sam said.

The next day was Friday. That evening the Gardners packed their car. They left early the next morning.

It took them seven days to see fourteen barns. Sam did the driving, while Barbara navigated. Every time they'd approach a barn, she'd say, "Oh, my goodness, would you look at that! A round barn. Imagine that! Boys, look at the round barn. Say, you don't see those much anymore." Then she'd turn and smile at Sam. "You're right, Sam. This is a lot more interesting than the Museum of Science and Industry."

They camped at night, sleeping in a tent. Sam had forgotten the cots, so they had to sleep on the ground. It rained every night. Each evening, Barbara would crawl into her sleeping bag, sigh, and say, "Just think, we could be staying in a hotel right now. Instead, we're out here with nature. You were right, Sam, this is so much nicer. I bet we'll never forget this."

Sam kept quiet, having decided the first day that turning the other cheek was the higher, nobler path.

They would lie in the dark, listening to the rain pounding on the tent, a fine mist settling upon them. After a half hour, just as Sam was falling asleep, she would say, "Maybe next year we can visit the rest of those hardware stores."

They pulled into their driveway late Friday evening. The boys were asleep. They carried them up to their bedroom, took off their clothes and shoes, and put them in bed. Sam unloaded the car, while Barbara took a long bath.

Sam took a shower down in the basement in the "guy" shower, next to the furnace, with all the spiders. When he came upstairs, Barbara was lying in bed. She lifted up the covers for him. He sniffed the sheets. "It's good to be home," he said.

Barbara sighed. "I should have been nice," she said.

He was going to agree with her, but his pastoral judgment prevailed and he kept quiet.

"Are you mad at me?" she asked.

He was a little, but didn't think it would help matters to say so. Instead, he reached over and pulled her to him and they slid together into the trough in the middle of their bed. "If you turn over, I'll give you a back rub," he said.

He was good for about five minutes, then he fell asleep. There was a time when being alone with his wife in bed would have kept him sufficiently excited to stay awake, but that was fourteen barns and six nights in a leaky tent ago. Now he just wanted to sleep.

Barbara lay awake, listening to his breathing and thinking. He was getting more like his father, more inclined to tell her how things were going to be. But he generally came around, if she gave him time. In most ways, he was a good husband. Whenever she put on a dress and asked him if she looked fat, he always said, "You are as slender as the day we were married." Though it wasn't true, the way he said it made it seem as if he believed it.

She regretted her sarcasm. They'd been married twelve years. He had his faults. She had heard his jokes dozens of times. He was losing his hair. He would stand in front of the mirror each morning combing his hair and ask her, "Am I getting bald?" She would say, "You are as handsome as the day we met." Which didn't answer his question, but he would smile just the same.

After twelve years, the illusions of hoped-for perfection have died. But when your expectations have been adjusted and you can still love each other, you're doing well, Barbara thought. Sam wasn't everything she thought he would be. But in some ways he was better. She was trying hard to remember that. And if he turned out to be like his father, that wouldn't be so bad. After all, his father had his good points. He'd taught Sam to stand when she'd entered the room, to hold the door, and tell her she was as beautiful as the day they were married. If Sam turned out to be like him, that wouldn't be all bad, would it?

Eleven

Signs and Wonders

While on the Gardners' vacation tour of all the round barns in the state, Sam took a careful inventory of the church signs they'd passed. He counted nine *Come Grow With Us!* signs, three instances of *If You Think It's Hot Down Here . . .* , and one *God Is Coming Soon And Boy, Is She Mad!* at an Episcopalian church. Another sign predicted the end of the world was at hand, but if it didn't end by the following Friday everyone was cordially invited to the ham-and-bean fund-raising dinner.

The sign in front of Harmony Friends Meeting is comparatively straightforward. It lists the times for Sunday school and worship, notes that Sam Gardner is the pastor, and reminds passersby that each Tuesday morning the Friendly Women's Circle gathers to make noodles.

There was a discussion at the August elders meeting whether the sign should say

157

more. Dale Hinshaw suggested using the sign as a tool of evangelism, perhaps posting a different verse each week from the book of Revelation that might cause people to consider their walk with the Lord. The Friendly Women's Circle proposed using the sign to advertise their annual Chicken Noodle Dinner, while Bill Muldock thought it might be nice to list the church's Heavenly Hoops basketball schedule on the sign.

Sam was horrified at the prospect of seeing any of that on the sign, so he hid the letters for the sign in the meetinghouse attic behind the box of Christmas decorations. He told Frank, the secretary, that if Dale came snooping around looking for the letters, to tell him he hadn't seen them.

"Wouldn't that be lying?" Frank asked.

"Did you actually see me put the letters in the attic?"

"No."

"Then it's not lying."

Sam has been wanting to put up his own sign. After fifteen years of pastoring Quaker meetings and sitting through endless meetings marked by discord and indecision, he wants to post a sign that reads, *Tired of Organized Religion? Try Us.* But he feared the subtlety of his point might be lost.

Back in May, at the Mighty Men of God

Conference, Dale Hinshaw had attended a church-growth workshop presented by a pastor from Iowa who had taken a church of twenty-three people and built it up to nine hundred by the strategic placement of Scripture verses throughout the church building. He'd written a book about his triumph, in which he revealed his secrets for convicting unbelievers and putting people in their place. Dale bought three copies.

Listening to the preacher from Iowa talk about convicting the unbelievers made Dale wish Sam was harder on sin. Sam never talks about convicting the unbelievers. Dale suspects Sam has never really given his heart to the Lord. Dale asked him the specific date he became a Christian and Sam said he wasn't sure, that he'd just grown up in the church and had always been a Christian.

"But you gotta have a definite date when you asked Jesus into your heart. Didn't you ever do that?" Dale persisted.

"I never asked him to leave my heart in the first place," Sam said.

This only added to Dale's doubts about Sam. He told his wife, "I don't know what's wrong with him. He don't even know the date he became a Christian."

Dolores Hinshaw frowned. "Well, what'd

you expect from someone who's strayed from the Word?"

Undaunted, Dale began posting Scripture admonitions around the meetinghouse. Over the sink in the kitchen he hung a sign reading: *You cleanse the outside of the cup and the dish, but inside you are full of extortion and wickedness! (Luke 11:39).* That did not go over with the Friendly Women's Circle, who like to think their noodles have brought untold thousands to the Lord. In the meetinghouse nursery, Dale placed a sober warning to the nursery workers: *Whoever causes one of these little ones who believe in me to sin, it would be better for him if a great millstone were hung round his neck and he were thrown into the sea (Mark 9:42).*

He posted James 3:1 over Sam's desk: *Let not many of you become teachers, for you know that we who teach shall be judged with greater strictness.* Sam had taken it down three times, so Dale burned it into the paneling with a woodburning kit while Sam was on vacation.

The final straw for Dale came in early September when Sam, without asking anyone's permission, got the letters for the meetinghouse sign out of the attic and wrote on the sign: *To dream of the person you wish to become is to waste the person you are.*

Dale had several problems with the sign, chief among them his conviction that Sam's sign violated the first point of the four-point plan of salvation: *Admit you are a sinner.* He bickered with Sam about it after church.

"We're not supposed to be happy with who we are," Dale said. "That's the whole point of going to church, so we can feel bad about who we are. Now you come along with this sign saying we don't need to change, that who we are is good enough, and it just gives people an excuse to keep on sinning. That's the dumbest sign I ever seen. Where'd you get that idea, anyway?"

Sam told him he'd seen it on vacation, in front of a Unitarian church.

"Well, there you go, that's what I mean. Unitarians wouldn't know the Lord if He was wearing a name tag."

Dale went on for another ten minutes, accusing Sam of turning the church into a hotbed of carnality with signs encouraging fornication.

"I never encouraged any such thing," Sam said.

"You certainly did. It's right there on the sign. To dream of the person you wish to become is to waste the person you are. What if what you are is a fornicator? You've just told people it's okay to keep being that way."

"That's not what the sign means, Dale, and you know it."

"Then you tell me what it means."

"Well, it means everyone is valuable, and we shouldn't waste our lives trying to be something or someone we're not."

Dale snorted. "I can't say I'm surprised. The Reverend Johnny LaCosta talked about this just the other day on his television show, how making our peace with sin will be the ruination of our country."

"What's wrong with people appreciating who they are, Dale?"

"Because who we are isn't good enough. Can't you see that? We're sinners. Why should we feel good about that?"

"Because that's not all we are," Sam said. "And, Dale, how do you think God feels when He creates someone, and they spend their entire lives wishing they were someone else. Isn't that being ungrateful?"

Dale frowned, concerned Sam might have a point. Then he brightened. "Matthew 5:48 says we're to be perfect as our heavenly Father is perfect." He beamed triumphantly. There was no finer feeling to Dale than hitting the bull's-eye with a Scripture arrow.

He drew a deep breath, girded his loins,

and plunged ahead. "Now, Jesus would never ask something of us if it weren't possible, so it must be possible to be perfect, which is what we have to strive for, even though we'll always be sinners. But if we ignore Jesus and don't aim for perfection, then we've proved our disobedience, which means we're still sinners deserving of hell. And it's all because we were content to be sinners and didn't care about perfection, which is why we shouldn't be happy with who we are and need to work hard to be someone else."

Sam tried to follow what he was saying, but by then had a pounding headache, which is how most of his conversations with Dale ended. He thought it'd probably just be easier to take down the sign and put up *Come Grow With Us!* or a verse from the book of Revelation.

"Why don't I just take down the sign?" Sam offered.

"That's being a good pastor, Sam. I knew you'd see my point, if you just put your mind to it."

Sam turned the lights off, closed up the meetinghouse, and walked home with Barbara and the boys. He was quiet.

"What's wrong, honey?" she asked, after a few blocks.

"Oh, nothing. I'm just tired," he said.

"Tired? We just got back from vacation. How could you be tired?"

How indeed?

The next day was Monday, Sam's day off. He went to the office anyway to change the sign. He didn't want Dale calling him at home, hounding him about it.

He rummaged around in his desk, looking for the key to the sign. "Hey, Frank, where's the sign key?"

"Don't ask me. I never did anything with it."

"Hmm, I'm sure I put it back in my desk the other day. But it's not here. Maybe I left it in my pants pocket."

He called home and asked Barbara if she'd found a key in his pants when she'd done the laundry.

"Nope, no key. I did find a tube of ChapStick, though. I've told you not to leave it in your pockets. It melts in the dryer and gets all over everything. I wish you wouldn't do that."

She paused, then chuckled. "Of course, my wishing you were different doesn't mean I'm not grateful for the person you are." She was laughing by now.

"Very funny," he said and hung up the phone. His own wife had turned on him.

"Don't we have a spare key for the sign?" Frank asked.

"Nope. It got lost last year, and we never had a spare key made."

"You know, Sam, I hope you don't take this wrong, but Pastor Jimmy over at the Harmony Worship Center really has his church organized. He has extra keys for all the locks and knows right where everything is. Maybe you should try to be a little more like him. Why'd you have to go and change the sign anyway? It was fine the way it was."

Sam had put the sign up because it was different, because it wasn't drivel, like all the other church signs he'd ever seen. *To dream of the person you wish to become is to waste the person you are.* Sam liked the feel of it.

All his life, people had told him who he was wasn't good enough, that he could be better, that he should admit he was a sinner. No one ever reminded him he was the light of the world, the salt of the earth, made in God's image. Dale never hung those Scripture verses around the meeting-house. After all, it might cause people to feel good about themselves, which would be dangerous. It might cause people to think they were worthy of love and, therefore, desirable, which would, of course, lead to fornication.

Sam searched another hour for the key, but couldn't find it.

"Well, I guess we'll just have to leave the sign up," he told Frank.

"We could always break the glass."

"No, I don't think so. The key'll turn up, and when it does, we'll change it then."

But he didn't plan to look very hard.

When Dale phoned later in the day to complain, Sam suggested that not finding the key to the sign was itself a sign from God. Then he added, "He who has ears, let him hear. Matthew 13:9." It was a beautiful moment for Sam, trumping Dale Hinshaw with a Scripture verse.

The sign is still there. Sam imagines some people genuinely appreciate it. They walk past, read it, and, for a brief moment, love themselves. They stop wishing they were someone else and thank God for making them who they are — a person worthy of love. Contrary to Dale's theory, there has not been an outbreak of fornication. If anything, in loving themselves, in reminding themselves that maybe they really are the light of the world, they have become a bit more holy, a bit more eager to gladden God's heart.

Every now and then, Sam observes from his office window as folks stop to read the sign. He watches their brows furrow in thought and slight smiles curve into place. In Sam's mind, they walk away a little straighter, their heads held a bit higher, an air of peace about them. The scolding inward voice reminding them of their deficiencies is silenced, if only for a moment. He wonders if, as they walk away they repeat the words to themselves, like a hymn, like a holy chant: *To dream of the person you wish to become is to waste the person you are.*

Sam is thinking of maybe preaching about it, just to give people a break. They come to church and sit through Dale Hinshaw's Sunday school class hearing that they're lower than worms, then trudge into the meeting room laden with shame. To learn God made them and declared them good might be a comfort.

Then again, it might make them mad. They'd accuse him of encouraging spiritual sloth. People who've been told all their lives they're not good enough get upset when anyone suggests otherwise. They believe grace ought be kept a secret, lest people take advantage of God's mercy and fall headlong into sin. That's the big fear. Sam could hear them now. "You won't be whistling the same tune when our teenage girls walk in here pregnant and the boys kill an usher and run off with the collection plate."

Sam wondered why it was if you told some people they were no-good sinners, they'd thank you for setting them straight and drop an extra twenty in the offering. But if you said God loved them just as they were, they'd go find a church where the preacher wasn't so liberal. Dale had told Sam about the church in Iowa that had grown to nine hundred people through scriptural admonitions. Sam was suspicious of any church that beat people down in order to lift God up.

It bothers Sam that all the church has done for some people is make them feel like rats. If there were a Unitarian church in town, he might just go. That would get people talking. It wasn't hard to imagine what Dale would say. "I knew he was a fraud when he couldn't tell me the date he became a Christian. Don't surprise me at all. He was fine up until he went to that seminary. That's where he got ruined, if you ask me."

The next time the budget came up for discussion, they'd take the thirty dollars they normally sent to the seminary and mail it to the church in Iowa instead, a true Christian organization that wasn't afraid to tell people how rotten they were, in order that they might know God's love and be saved.

Let them have their signs, Sam thought. He would have his. *To dream of the person you wish to become is to waste the person you are.*

Twelve

Bea

The Corn and Sausage Days parade has been a mainstay of the town since 1954, when it was first held. It's the same parade every year. There's no point in going to it again and again, though if you don't, people question your loyalty. Moving away is not a sufficient excuse for missing the parade. If you can make it home for your mother's funeral, you can come back for the parade, too. Unless you've gotten too good for this town, in which case no one was surprised and they're glad to see you gone. And good riddance.

The parade begins with the recitation of the town poem, written in 1898 by Miss Ora Crandell — librarian, thespian, and Harmony poet laureate.

> *O' Harmony, sweet Harmony,*
> *We lift our song of praise to thee.*
> *Whether far or whether near,*
> *In our hearts we hold you dear.*

170

In 1954, Vernon Hodge wrote a second verse paying tribute to the corn plant, the modest pig, and the Lord, which together have brought prosperity to the town and made it the Athens of the Midwest it is today.

> *O' mighty stalks and noble swine,*
> *We celebrate and laud,*
> *Making life so fair and fine,*
> *With a little help from God.*

The Sausage Queen recites the poem from memory, which is the chief requirement for being the Sausage Queen — the ability to look earnest and shed a tear while saying, "In our hearts, we hold you dear." Once crowned, the Sausage Queen must be an enthusiastic sausage consumer, which leaves the Sausage Queen, by the end of her reign, considerably broadened by her experiences.

There is no bathing suit competition in the Sausage Queen contest, this being a Christian town opposed to the inflammation of male passions. Though to be truthful, most of the Sausage Queens could not have inflamed male passions in a prison, with the exception of the 1974 Sausage Queen, Nora Nagle, who was pure beauty and moved to New York where she starred in a Boraxo commercial.

In January, the Sausage Queen goes on to the state contest in the city, where she gives a speech on the benefits of pork consumption and talks about what an honor it would be to represent the state in the national Sausage Queen contest, and how her faith in God has brought her this far, so no matter what happens, she is confident something good will come of it, and how, in meeting the other Sausage Queens, she's made friends she'll have the rest of her life and she just thanks God she lives in a country where they have the freedom to be Sausage Queens or anything at all they want to be. Then she gives a little curtsy, people clap, and she cries, then steps aside so the other ninety-one Sausage Queens can say the exact same thing.

What has everyone talking this year is that Nora Nagle, of Boraxo fame, has come back home to live and was invited to ride in Harvey Muldock's Cranbrook with this year's Sausage Queen, who was a little miffed at having to share the glory, but smiled and waved anyway, like it didn't bother her a bit.

In 1975, Nora Nagle went on to be crowned the state Sausage Queen, which she parlayed into a career on stage and screen. In addition to the Boraxo commercial, she was a dancing grape in an underwear commercial. Then she was hired as a stuntwoman on the set of *Charlie's Angels*, where she drove a car over a cliff, fell from a hotel balcony into a swimming pool, and was struck over the head with a chair.

When Farrah Fawcett left the show, Nora auditioned for the opening and would have gotten it, except for the permanently dazed expression on her face from being hit with the chair. Instead, they hired Cheryl Ladd (born Cheryl Jean Stoppelmoor in Huron, South Dakota), which Nora believes was God closing a door to open a window, though God hasn't gotten around to opening the window just yet.

Being hit in the head with the chair was the high point of Nora's career. It went downhill from there, which would have discouraged a lesser person, but Sausage Queens are resilient and bounce back quickly from adversity.

She's working at Kivett's Five and Dime as a cashier, which she believes is only temporary. Her agent will be calling any day with news of her big break, but until then she's happy to be home, where she can remember her roots and draw strength from the people who launched her career.

In 1975, when she won the state Sausage Queen contest, the town board voted to rename Main Street the Nora Nagle Boulevard, but the street department dawdled around and didn't change the street signs. Now that her career's gone belly-up, everyone is grateful for their inefficiency. It would have been awkward having Main Street named after a cashier.

In addition to working at Kivett's Five and Dime, Nora has written a play, formed a community theater group, and secured the Royal Theater for the debut of *Nora: A Sausage Queen Remembers. A no-holds-barred exposé of my life in the film industry* read the poster she taped to the display window of the Royal Theater.

Nora: A Sausage Queen Remembers was the topic of conversation around town the week of the parade. Mostly because Sam Gardner, a man of the cloth, had joined the community theater group.

"Probably to snuggle up to that Nora Nagle vixen," Dale Hinshaw said to his wife. He was giving serious thought to standing during worship and urging Sam to repent and separate himself from the taint of the carnal world.

The town was of two minds on the play. The men at the barbershop talked about the importance of culture and thought they probably should attend the no-holds-barred exposé of Nora's life in the film industry, purely in the interests of art and citizenship.

"I don't really want to go," Kyle Weathers said. "I have other things to do. But I realize it's not always about what I want."

The ladies of the Friendly Women's Circle at Harmony Friends Meeting weren't as civic-minded.

"It sounds like filth to me," Fern Hampton said. "A no-holds-barred exposé. I bet she ends up naked as a jaybird and prancing around on that stage. You watch and see."

But what really set the Friendly Women's teeth on edge was that *Nora: A Sausage Queen Remembers* was scheduled for the same day as their annual Chicken Noodle Dinner.

"Now people will have to choose between coming here for our wholesome chicken and noodles or going to the theater to see her smutty little play, and what do you think they'll choose? Smut, that's what!" said Bea Majors. "I think Satan's behind this. He'd just love to see our Chicken Noodle Dinner flop. That'd be a feather in his cap for sure."

Bea is the town's resident expert on Satanic activity, having volunteered as a devil watcher for the Reverend Johnny LaCosta's television ministry. For a hundred-dollar donation, Bea was allowed the privilege of spying out the devil's handiwork and notifying the Reverend, who would then expose the devil on national television and foil the Tempter's snare.

He had sent Bea a pamphlet listing thirty-eight signs of Satanic activity, the third clue being nudity. According to Johnny LaCosta, if someone's naked, Satan is lurking in the vicinity. The Reverend advises true Christians to bathe in body-length bathing suits. He believes if Bathsheba had been attired more modestly the devil could never have entered King David's heart and gotten him in all that trouble. For a love offering of three hundred dollars, the Reverend will send you a body-length bathing suit that he himself has touched, thereby thwarting Satan's advances.

Bea was torn. She couldn't decide whether to attend *Nora: A Sausage Queen Remembers* in order to spy out Satanic activity or bring people to the Lord through the Friendly Women's Circle chicken noodle ministry. She sat in her living room, praying for a divine nudge. Then she flipped on the television, and there was Johnny LaCosta preaching from the sixteenth chapter of Romans about keeping an eye on those who caused dissension and offense.

Well, if that didn't describe Nora right down to her slingback pumps, Bea didn't know what did.

The Reverend was in a tizzy. He certainly didn't mean to contradict Paul or add words to Scripture, but Paul probably hadn't anticipated how bad things would get. It wasn't enough to keep an eye on evildoers, the Reverend said. The Christian must be prepared to take charge, intervene, and nip Satan's follies in the bud. He urged his television audience to become bud-nippers for the Lord, but warned them to be careful — that the world didn't like bud-nippers and they'd face persecution.

That's when Bea realized her obligation — she had to take charge, attend the play, and nip Satan's buds when the clothes started flying. Though honored to be called to such a noble mission, she was a little fearful. What if the community theater group rose against her? What if they killed her and used her body in a ritual Satanic sacrifice? She thought of turning back, but when you've pledged to be a bud-nipper for the Lord, there can be no retreat. To be on the safe side, she left a note on her kitchen table saying that if anything happened to her, people should look for her body in Nora's crawl space.

Bea was the first to arrive at the theater. She watched from the front row as the group rehearsed. Pitiful dimwits, all of them, Bea thought. Soft-headed people vulnerable to manipulation. And there was her minister, right in the thick of it.

Nora was speaking to Sam. "Now remember, Sam, you're playing the part of a Hollywood director. So when I ask what I have to do to be in your movie, you pat the couch and say, 'Come sit beside me and we'll talk about it.' Then I'll say my lines and do some things, the lights will dim, and the scene will end."

Bea trembled with pious fervor. She'd be right there, in the front row when the clothes started flying, ready to take charge and slam the door in the devil's face. She wished the Reverend Johnny LaCosta were here to watch her. He'd be so proud.

The theater began filling. Bea glanced back, scanning the audience to see who was there. It was mostly men, many of whose wives were at that moment laboring in the vineyards of the Chicken Noodle Dinner. Bea was sickened by the depravity. Filthy men out to get their jollies while their saintly wives toiled to bring salvation to the hungry masses. She wished she'd brought her camera to photograph these supposedly Christian men and publish their pictures in the newspaper. There were other men there she didn't recognize. Rough-looking characters. Probably from the city, Bea thought.

Sam's scene was near the end of the play. So far everyone had kept on their clothes, but Bea knew it was only a matter of time. The third act ended, the curtain closed, there were shuffling noises backstage, and then the curtain opened again. Sam was onstage, sitting on a red velvet couch. A gold chain hung around his neck, and his shirt was unbuttoned at the top, his chest hairs plainly visible. A cigar dangled from his mouth.

There was a knock on a door.

"Come in," Sam barked.

Nora entered the stage with a flourish, talking about her dream of being an actress and how she'd starred in two commercials and was almost a Charlie's Angel. She then turned to Sam, the Hollywood director, and asked, "So what do I have to do to be in your movie?"

Sam patted the couch, then said, "Come sit beside me and we'll talk about it."

All the men in the theater leaned forward. This was it, the payoff, their reward for sitting through three numbing hours of Nora recalling her torturous climb up the Hollywood ladder.

Bea wanted to close her eyes, but didn't. She edged forward, ready to bud-nip. Lord, give me strength to do your will, she prayed.

Nora moved toward Sam, then said, "I won't do it. I know what you're after, but I'm not that kind of girl."

The men groaned. This was no better than church.

Then Nora talked about how two roads diverged in the woods and how she had taken the one less traveled back to her hometown. She'd gone away to find success, and some people thought she'd failed, but she hadn't. Because success wasn't about being famous or rich or beautiful. It was about friendship and love and helping others, which people could do no matter where they lived.

A morality play wasn't quite what Bea expected, and truthfully she was a little put out. She'd worked up the courage to be a bud-nipper, only to discover Nora was a decent human being after all.

Unfortunately, Bea wasn't the only one disappointed. The man sitting behind her yelled that he wanted his money back, that he'd paid to see a no-holds-barred exposé.

The other men started grumbling. Three hours and seven dollars down the drain. It was turning ugly.

Nora began to weep.

Bea leaped to her feet, two hundred and twenty-three pounds of bottled-up righteous indignation in search of a target, and said, "You want no-holds-barred? I'll give you no-holds-barred." She swung her purse at the man, striking him on the head. Then she hurried up the stairs, gathered Nora in her arms, and hustled her off the stage to safety.

That was the picture Bob Miles from the *Harmony Herald* ran in the newspaper — Bea Majors throwing herself toward Nora, above the caption *Local Women Involved in Movie House Altercation*. There was no further explanation, no mention of Bea coming to Nora's rescue. With the Chicken Noodle Dinner and the Corn and Sausage Days parade to report on, there wasn't room for details.

Beneath the picture and caption was an editorial, written by Bob's wife, Arvella, lamenting the decline of civilization and congratulating those Friendly Women who labored to better their community through the Chicken Noodle Dinner. She listed all the women who'd made the dinner the success it was. Bea's name was conspicuously absent.

Bea read the paper while sitting in her kitchen soaking her feet. The Reverend Johnny LaCosta had it all figured out, she thought. It is a dangerous thing to be a bud-nipper for the Lord. The world will despise you. At first she was discouraged, but not for long. What mattered was that God knew her heart.

Even when Fern Hampton told her she'd brought shame to the Circle, Bea wasn't troubled. She didn't bother to defend herself. She told Fern, "Don't think you know the whole story, because you don't." Rich irony, coming from Bea, but if she could learn it, so could Fern.

Meanwhile, Bea is thinking of joining Nora's community theater group. They are a sad and sorry lot. Pitiful dimwits, all of them, who sat like lumps on logs while Nora was under attack. They need leadership, someone who knows something about taking charge. Someone who can fight the good fight. Someone like Bea.

Thirteen
Persistence

With the Chicken Noodle Dinner over for the year, life at Harmony Friends Meeting has returned to normal. Frank, the secretary, has gone back to being his usual grouchy self. For three weeks he had to be polite when people phoned the meetinghouse asking when the dinner was and what exactly it was they would be serving.

"Well, it's still the second Saturday in September, the same as it's been since 1964. And since it's a chicken noodle dinner, I'd say we're serving chicken and noodles. But that's just a wild guess. I might be wrong."

That's what he wanted to say. Instead he had to be polite and tell them the date and the serving hours and that, in addition to the chicken and noodles, the ladies would also be serving Tastee bread with one pat of butter, orange Jell-O with carrot slivers and pineapple, and your choice of cake or pie for dessert.

Frank believes this whole chicken noodle business has gotten out of hand, that the women of the Circle are using it as leverage to get their way. The dinner is the biggest moneymaker for the church. When the meeting was slow about buying a new stove for the meetinghouse kitchen, the women let it be known that the Baptists had invited them to move the dinner there.

"They've offered us a new stove, another noodle freezer, and six new tea pitchers," Fern Hampton said during the monthly business meeting. "We've been telling you for years we need new tea pitchers, but nothing's been done. Now we need a new stove, and you'll dilly-dally about that and one day it'll explode and that'll be the end of the Friendly Women."

We should be so lucky, Frank thought to himself.

The stove was purchased in 1953 in memory of Mrs. Ralph Hobbs, the founder of the Happy Helpmates Sunday school class, who for over thirty years trained the young ladies of the meeting how to submit to their husbands, manage a Christian home, and make noodles. The first two lessons hadn't stuck, but they'd mastered the noodles.

In 1953, the stove was the top of the line.

Cast-iron, six burners, and two ovens. But it's not worked right since 1967, when the late Juanita Harmon turned the gas on, went in search of a match, discovered they were out, walked three blocks to the Kroger to buy a box of matches, returned a half hour later, struck an Ohio Blue Tip to light the pilot, and died a martyr in service to the Lord. When the oven door is open, you can see the faint outline of her startled face.

People still talk about her funeral. The Friendly Women served as pallbearers and folded a ceremonial apron at graveside, which they presented to Juanita's husband, who said, "She was book smart, but never had much common sense," which pretty well summed up the feelings of everyone present.

They wanted to buy a new stove in 1967, but Juanita Harmon's sister, Alice, was of the opinion the stove should remain in the kitchen as a memorial to her fallen sibling and got her knickers in a twist whenever anyone suggested replacing it. But in late September, Alice's niece from California came to town for a visit, took one look at Alice, and shipped her off to the nursing home in Cartersburg. The next Sunday, Fern Hampton, with the Alice roadblock now removed, ordered the meeting to cough up a new stove or else.

"Three of the burners don't work, the oven burns everything, and we can't get new parts. Buy us a new one, or we're moving the dinner to the Baptist church."

Harvey Muldock suggested maybe he could fix the stove.

Fern snorted. "You've been saying that since 1967. We're tired of waiting."

The veterans of the church wars began trembling in their folding chairs. This was reminiscent of the Great Pew Cushion Battle of 1948, which had led to the Great Quaker Migration of 1949 — all twenty-three members of the Darnell family packed their wagons and moved west to the Methodist church.

Ten years later, Harry Darnell hit it big in the concrete business, building thousands of bomb shelters across five states. When he died in 1981, he left half a million dollars to the Methodist church. It still rankled the Quakers that that money could have been theirs if Fern Hampton's mother, Fleeta, had backed off and let Thelma Darnell pick the color of the new pew cushions. But the Hampton women do not have a reverse gear. It is not in their nature to retreat. Thelma Darnell wanted purple cushions, symbolizing our Lord's Resurrection. But Fleeta Hampton wanted the orange pew cushions, which were thirty dollars cheaper, but ultimately cost the meeting half a million dollars.

The Methodists used the money to build a gymnasium and buy a stove with eight burners, an irony several people were aching to point out to Fern, but didn't for the sake of Christian charity.

The silver lining of Juanita Harmon's explosive demise was the Juanita Harmon Memorial Fund — a one-thousand-dollar certificate of deposit on ice since 1967, now worth six thousand dollars. With Alice banished to the nursing home, unable to guard her sister's reputation, thirty-five years of repressed anger boiled to the surface.

"We wouldn't be in this mess if she'd just used her head," Fern said. "I say we take the money out of her fund."

Miriam Hodge pointed out the Juanita Harmon Memorial Fund was a designated fund, to be used solely for mission purposes.

Fern frowned at Miriam. "Well, Miriam, if you want to be legalistic, I suppose you're technically correct. Though I think there's something to be said for being open to the Lord's leading."

Then she cautioned those present against being like the Pharisees and said she was grateful God had given her a spirit of freedom so she could follow his glorious will, which was to see a new stainless-steel, two-oven, eight-burner stove installed in the meetinghouse kitchen.

It was a moment rich in irony. Fern Hampton, a stalwart guardian of religious law, magically transformed into the Patrick Henry of spiritual liberty.

Miriam let it drop. She was hoping Sam would object, but sensing conflict, he'd excused himself ten minutes earlier to use the rest room, where he'd locked the stall door and sat quietly reading a book until the meeting was finished. The secret of pastoral longevity is knowing when to use the restroom and for how long.

"So what'd they decide about the stove?" he asked Barbara on the way home from church.

"They've formed a Stove Committee to pick out a new one."

"Who's on the committee?" Sam asked.

"Fern Hampton and three other women. They named you as the fifth person in case they can't agree and need you to decide."

Sam flinched. He had a fleeting vision of the entire church locked in a heated debate over the merits of gas stoves versus electric stoves. Entire families would leave the church. Fifty years from now, people would still be talking about the Great Stove Battle.

Who was the pastor then? they'd ask.

"Some fella named Sam Gardner. They got ridda him and the last anyone heard he was selling used cars up in the city."

Sam wondered if he should just resign now and get it over with.

Fern called him later that afternoon. "We're going up to the city tomorrow to look at stoves. We'll be past to pick you up around seven. Be ready."

"Gee, Fern, I don't know. Tomorrow's my day off and I was counting on doing something with Barbara."

"Bring her along then, just so she knows she doesn't get a vote."

Quakers don't actually vote on church matters, preferring to gather in silence, reflect on God's will, and act accordingly. This theological subtlety has been lost on Fern, who believes the meeting has gathered to learn her will and act accordingly.

They visited three stove stores before finding one that offered a discount to churches, which in the end wouldn't have mattered anyway. No matter how much they paid, someone was sure to stand at the next monthly business meeting and say, "Well, I just wished I'd known about this. I got a cousin in Ohio who can get these stoves for next to nothin'. I just wished someone woulda told me."

That would have led to a two-hour discussion on the business procedures of the meeting, examining whether they were doing everything they could to keep people informed. They'd end up forming a new committee to evaluate and, if necessary, modify the church's decision-making process. The committee would never meet, but a year later they'd have the same problem and someone would say, "I thought we formed a committee to look at this." Then they would argue whether a committee had actually been formed and if so, why hadn't it met, and someone would suggest maybe it was time to form a committee to find out what had happened. They would nod their heads sagely, agree it was a fine idea, and appoint a committee. Tired, though pleased to be of service to the Lord, they would adjourn the meeting, go home, and eat pot roast.

The new stove was delivered the next Monday. The Friendly Women were present, overseeing, as three burly men from the stove store pulled the old cast-iron stove out from the wall, muscled it onto a dolly, and headed for the kitchen door. It got stuck halfway through. They pushed harder, which lodged it even tighter. The men began to swear, under their breath at first, in deference to their surroundings, but then louder and more fervently.

"How'd you get it in here in the first place?" they asked.

The ladies weren't sure. Then Opal Majors, recalling the Juanita Harmon Inferno of 1967, said, "They rebuilt that wall after the stove exploded. I told 'em then the new door wasn't wide enough to ever get the stove out, but they told me not to worry, that the stove would last another fifty years, and then it'd be someone else's problem."

This pretty well summarized the philosophy of Harmony Friends Meeting. *If you do it right the first time, there will be nothing for your children and grandchildren to do.* So there they were, with a new stove they couldn't get in and an old stove they couldn't remove. Compliments of their ancestors, whose service to the Lord had only succeeded in creating more problems than it had ever solved.

They called Sam from the kitchen phone, who reminded them it was his day off. He'd worked two weeks without a break and was irritated. "What do you want me to do about it? Lay my hands on it and pray it through the door? There's nothing I can do. Tell 'em to hook the old stove back up and haul the new one back to the store."

That they would not do. It had taken them thirty-five years and sixty-eight committee meetings to get their brand-new stainless-steel, two-oven, eight-burner stove. Now the only thing keeping them from victory was eight inches of wood and drywall. But they couldn't count on the men from the church. Sam had proven that. Faced with a great struggle, the men would form yet another committee and recommend fixing the old stove. They would blanch in the face of battle. Meanwhile, the Promised Land was just over the ridge, perched in the back of the truck, its oven doors gleaming in the autumn sun.

Fern ordered the men to pull the old stove back into the kitchen, which they did. She commanded the Friendly Women to fall in. They stretched out in a line across the kitchen, a human wall of grit and determination.

She strode back and forth in front of them, recalling their past hardships: the Juanita Harmon Inferno of 1967, the Noodle Depression of 1975, the Coffeemaker Catastrophe of 1986, the Crosley Freezer Failure of 1999.

"We've overcome hard times before," she said. "We can do it again."

She ordered them to return to the kitchen

in a half hour, armed with their electric knives. "Do not tell your husbands. They will only discourage you."

A half hour later, the women reassembled in the kitchen. They cleaned and oiled their electric knives, readying their weapons for battle. Fern gave the command, and they plugged in their knives and began to saw through the door frame as if it were a turkey at Thanksgiving, one thin slice at a time. The knives would clog, the women would fall to the floor exhausted, only to be dragged away as fresh troops took their place. Miriam Hodge nicked an electrical wire, sparks flew, and the smell of ozone filled the air. Opal Majors cut her finger, but stayed in the trenches, oblivious to the pain, her blood dripping onto the linoleum.

The stove men sat watching, enthralled, knowing better than to utter a word.

Finally, the opening was large enough. The men rose to help. Fern glared at them. "Stay put. This is not about you. This is not your fight." The women loaded the old stove on the dolly and wheeled it to the truck. They then carried the new stove through the door, lowered it into place, hooked up the gas, and fired the burners.

Sam came in just as they were finishing. He surveyed the opening, then spied the electric knife blades scattered on the floor, bent and dulled, among spatters of Opal's blood. He grew pale at the carnage, turned, and fled. The women snorted. They weren't surprised. Men didn't have the stomach for battle. They talked a good game, but that was all. They formed committees, held conventions where they pontificated and blustered, and then maybe wrote a book on why something couldn't be done.

But if you wanted to cross the finish line, it took the tenacity of a Friendly Woman. For victory belongs not to the wisest, nor to the strongest, but to the persistent. The trophy goes not to the hare, but to the tortoise, who, never stopping to rest, plods ahead, her eye always on the prize.

Fourteen
Deadline

Bob Miles, Sr., passed away the first weekend in October. His son, Bob Jr., hadn't heard from him since late Friday. So Monday morning, on his way to work at the *Herald*, he stopped past his father's house and found him reclining in his La-Z-Boy, beyond resuscitation. His hand lay limp in a bowl of Chee-tos. His face was colorless, except for a ring of Chee-to orange around his mouth.

Bob's first feeling was one of relief. With his father gone, he'd no longer have to go by "Bob Junior." Now he could be just plain "Bob." His second feeling was guilt that his first feeling had been relief. His third feeling was regret. He and his father had never gotten along. Bob had been meaning to patch things up, but was a little too late. One more newspaper editor who'd missed a deadline.

Bob lifted his father's hand out of the Chee-tos, wet a washcloth at the bathroom sink, and cleaned the orange from around his father's mouth. Then he combed Bob Sr.'s hair, brushed the Chee-to crumbs from his shirt, and phoned Johnny Mackey at the funeral home to come with his hearse.

While Bob was waiting for Johnny to show, he nosed around the house. There was a Sunday bulletin from the Baptist church on the kitchen table, which meant his father had died sometime after church. Unless he'd died on Saturday, missed church, and a deacon on his visitation rounds, mistaking Bob's death for slumber, had tiptoed past Bob and laid the bulletin on the table.

Although that wouldn't reflect well on the Baptist visitation program, the awareness of someone's mortality being a crucial element to a successful visit, it was not without precedent. In 1956, Grace Mills sat dead under a hair dryer at Laverne's Beauty Shop for seven hours before anyone grew suspicious. Fortunately, the heat from the hair dryer had kept her limber, and they were able to display her in an open casket at her funeral. In fairness to Laverne and her customers, it had been an understandable oversight — Grace Mills had appeared lifeless for years.

While Bob was reading the church bulletin, the doorbell rang. When he opened the door, there stood Johnny Mackey in his black undertaker's suit. Bob noticed a pickup in the driveway.

"Where's the hearse?" he asked.

Johnny Mackey reddened. "In the shop. We'll need to use the truck."

Bob shook his head. "We're not hauling my father across town in a pickup truck like some piece of lumber."

"Bob, I know exactly how you feel, and I'm sorry as can be. But it could be a couple days before I get the hearse back, and I don't think we should wait that long." He lowered his voice and leaned closer toward Bob to confide an unpleasant truth. "If we wait too much longer, it's not going to smell very nice."

Bob sighed. "This is ridiculous. I can't believe this is happening."

"I'm sorry."

"Well, I guess it can't be helped. But I don't want him riding in the back. He'll ride up front in the cab with us."

It helped a little that the pickup truck was a new one, not some rust bucket with a dog in the back like all the other trucks in town. Bob tried to act as if nothing were amiss, as if driving down Main Street in a pickup truck with his dead father leaning into him was a common occurrence.

Johnny pulled into the garage of the funeral home and shut off the engine. His hands shook slightly; he removed the keys with a faint jingling. An old-man tremor, Bob thought. He noticed liver spots on Johnny's hands, then observed his silver hair. He'd always thought of Johnny Mackey as having black hair. He wondered when it had changed.

Johnny looked like he wanted to say something, but was hesitating.

"Uh, say, Bob, if you wouldn't mind, could you help me carry your father in? Ordinarily, I have a helper, but he's out sick today. If you could help me get him in, I can take it from there."

Since the likely alternative to not helping was Johnny Mackey dropping his father on the garage floor, Bob eased his dad out of the truck, his hands under his arms, while Johnny lifted his legs. They placed him on a gurney and wheeled him through the garage, up the ramp, and into the embalming room, where they lifted him from the cart and lowered him onto the porcelain embalming table.

"There we go. I can take it from here," Johnny said. "Thank you for your help, Bob. Sorry I had to ask. Used to be I could do this by myself."

"That's okay, Johnny. I didn't mind."

In an odd sort of way, he hadn't minded. It had eased his regrets for not patching things up with his father, which likely wouldn't have happened anyway. His father had never been the type to make up, preferring to stoke the fires of discord to a white-hot heat. Had he been alive, he'd have refused Bob's help. "Get away from me. Keep your hands offa me. I can walk in there myself."

It occurred to Bob that carrying his father into the funeral home was the first time he'd done something for him without his father pointing out he was doing it the wrong way. Still, Bob wouldn't have been surprised if his father had revived long enough to yell, "You don't lift a dead person that way. You gotta lift with your knees. Whadya tryin' to do? Give yourself a hernia? For cryin' out loud, use your head."

He walked around the corner and down the street to the *Herald* building, where he phoned his wife, Arvella, to tell her what had happened. She cried at first, then began to talk about how his death was actually a blessing.

"He hadn't been happy for the past few years," she told Bob. It was an understatement of huge proportion, implying Bob Miles, Sr., had been happy at one time.

This is the customary response to death in Harmony, to look on the bright side, to suggest someone's death was actually a stroke of wonderful luck, an immense good fortune.

When Grace Mills died under the hair dryer, it took Laverne exactly five minutes to make the cheerful observation that at least Grace already had her hair done for her funeral.

Bob sat at his desk, rolled a piece of paper into his Corona, and began to type his father's obituary:

ROBERT J. MILES, SR.

Robert J. Miles, Sr., editor emeritus of the *Harmony Herald* newspaper, passed away at his home. The editor of the *Herald* from 1945 to 1990, he was known for his conservative perspective.

Born on April 20, 1920, to Robert and Martha Miles, he was preceded in death by his wife, the former Rosemary Jenkins, whom he married in 1941. They had one son, Robert J. Miles, Jr., born in 1948, the current editor of the *Herald*.

A member of the Harmony First Baptist Church and the John Birch Society, he also founded the Live Free or Die

Sunday school class at Harmony Friends Meeting.

Services will be held Thursday at 10:00 A.M. at the Mackey Funeral Parlor.

Bob Sr. had founded the Live Free or Die Sunday school class in 1960 as a vehicle to air his bigotry. Now the class was taught by Dale Hinshaw, who used it to rail against homosexuals, Californians, and people who scoffed at the Rapture.

Founding the Live Free or Die Sunday school class had been Bob Sr.'s one burst of innovation. Like most cranks, he seldom initiated anything himself, preferring to shout advice from the bleachers. Bob's earliest memory was of his father sitting by the radio yelling at Harry Truman to drop the atom bomb on Korea. "Kill 'em all, that's what I say. Nothin' but a bunch of slant-eyed communists, the whole lot of 'em." This was the Robert J. Miles, Sr., strategy for foreign relations — kill everyone who didn't look and think like him — which he'd trumpeted across the editorial page of the *Herald* for forty-five years.

Bob was tempted, while writing the obituary, to put a positive spin on his father's life and make up something nice to say. It was pure habit, having expended much ink over the years trying to persuade people his father wasn't as bad as he seemed.

"Although it is true the editor emeritus, Robert Miles, Sr., wrote in last week's edition of the *Herald* that homosexuals ought to be put on a boat and sunk, we believe he meant that in a Christian sort of way."

But with his father dead, Bob no longer felt the need to follow behind him cleaning up his messes. Besides, he was weary of defending a man whose views were indefensible. He rolled the paper out of the typewriter and set it on the stack of copy for that week's edition of the paper.

It occurred to Bob he'd spent much of his life searching for some noble quality or virtue in his father. He'd even agreed to take over the *Herald* in hopes it might draw them together. But proximity to Robert Miles, Sr., had never deepened anyone's affection for him, and they'd had fierce arguments. In 1992, Bob had a plaque engraved recognizing his father as the editor emeritus, which he presented to his father at a surprise retirement party. After the party, he escorted his father to the office door, expressing his sincere desire that his father's retirement be filled with happiness, nudged him out the door, and phoned Uly Grant to come over and change the locks.

After that, his father wrote the editorials only when Bob was on vacation, which meant Bob had to spend his first week back apologizing for his father and clarifying his more strident comments.

"Though it is true the editor emeritus of this paper referred to the Democratic nominee for town council as a 'drug-snorting, free-love hippie' in last week's edition, we are confident he meant nothing personally by it."

He wondered if anyone would come to the funeral. His father hadn't had any real friends. There were a few men down at the Coffee Cup who'd passed the time with him, but they weren't the kind of men to put on a suit and attend a funeral. The most they would do was mention something to Bob the next time they saw him.

"Say, I heard about your father. He was a character, that's for sure."

Bob wished he had a dollar for every time someone had said to him, "Your father, I don't know about him. He sure is a . . ." They would pause to think up a suitable description, not wishing to insult a man's father, but neither wanting to adorn him with false praise. "A character," they'd invariably say, after several awkward seconds.

Bob imagined himself at the funeral,

shaking hands with people while they pointed out he'd been sired by a character. He wondered if maybe they could skip the funeral altogether and have a private showing, like they did for movie stars and war criminals.

His father had attended Harmony Friends until two years before, when Sam Gardner, in a rare display of backbone, had taken Bob Sr. to task for his behavior, which had resulted in Bob Sr.'s storming off to the Baptists. Sam had asked the elders if he should apologize and invite Bob Sr. to return, but the consensus was that they should quit while they were ahead.

Bob phoned the pastor of the Baptist church to see if he would conduct his father's funeral. He was sympathetic, clucking his tongue in all the right places. Then he told Bob he was leaving town the next day to attend a Mighty Men of God Conference in the city and suggested Bob give Sam Gardner a call.

Sam doesn't go to Mighty Men of God Conferences, or any kind of conference for that matter, after the Finance Committee took the money from his professional expense account to fix a leak in the meetinghouse roof. So when Bob called him to do the funeral, he was without an excuse and consequently stuck with the unenviable task of thinking up something nice to say about Robert Miles, Sr.

"Let's keep it simple," Bob suggested. "No showing. Just a funeral and a graveside service. Tell the Circle not to bother with a dinner."

Not that the Friendly Women's Circle would have bothered with a dinner anyway, having boycotted the *Herald* and Bob since March, when, on a slow news day, he'd written an editorial calling for an investigation of the Circle and their fund-raising efforts for Brother Norman's shoe ministry to the Choctaw Indians.

You do not dump on the Circle and then expect them to drop everything and whip up a funeral dinner in your hour of need. Atonement must be made, and forgiveness sought, which will not be granted, though it should be asked for nonetheless, in order to provide the ladies of the Circle one more opportunity to recall their disappointment with you.

The funeral was held on Thursday morning at ten o'clock. By nine forty-five, all the seats were taken, and Johnny Mackey and Sam had to carry extra chairs in from the garage. Bob Sr., it turns out, was a member of the Odd Fellows Lodge, which they hadn't remembered until Kyle Weathers pointed it out at the Monday night lodge meeting.

"Yeah, we joined the same day, April 16, 1977. He showed up a few times, then got mad and stopped comin'. But he's still a member. His name's on the books."

So the Odd Fellows turned out for the funeral in all their splendor, wearing their ceremonial sashes, and hijacked the proceedings, telling Sam it was their sacred obligation to honor their fallen brother. That was fine with Sam, since it meant he wouldn't have to stand at the lectern and lie about how they were better people for having known Bob Sr., but are grateful he's in a better place because he hadn't been happy for the past several years, so in that sense his death was a blessing.

Instead, Harvey Muldock went forward and repeated the Odd Fellows prayer, then talked about how in our Father's house were many Odd Fellow lodges, and that Bob Sr. had gone to prepare a place for them. He mentioned the last time he'd seen Bob Sr. alive, on Monday morning, riding through town with his son and Johnny Mackey in Johnny's pickup, and how Bob Sr. had seemed so full of life. Then, just that quick, like a snap of the fingers, he was gone. Harvey shook his head at the mystery of it.

They loaded Bob Sr. in the hearse, now in fine repair and sporting a fresh coat of wax, and drove to the cemetery on Lincoln Street across from the Co-op. The Odd Fellows bore him to his grave, then clustered around the tent. Sam read the Twenty-Third Psalm and said a prayer thanking God for sending them Bob Sr., trying not to sound too happy that the time had come to give him back.

People turned to look at Bob. He knew he should say something nice about his father, but nothing came. Fifty-some years he'd spent with his father and now he was unable to think up one good word to say. Nothing. Couldn't say his father had ever taken him fishing. Or played pitch and catch. Or tucked him in bed and told him he loved him.

"Uh, well, I appreciate you all being here. I know my father wasn't the easiest man to get along with. Not much pleased him."

Everyone looked at the ground.

Arvella tried to salvage the occasion. "He did like Chee-tos," she said.

People nodded their heads in agreement, then began drifting away from the tent in small clusters, discussing lunch plans.

This is what comes from not loving, Bob thought. You die and the nicest thing people can say about you is that you liked Chee-tos.

Bob has never been the kind of man to make solemn vows. But standing next to his father's casket, considering an empty hole and an emptier life, he pledged that by the time he died, there'd be something good to say about him.

Fifteen

Halloween

People have been gearing up for Halloween. Ned Kivett at the Five and Dime brought out the candy corn he didn't sell last Halloween and set it on the checkout counter, next to the plastic vampire teeth and fake blood. Amanda Hodge was selling pumpkins on the sidewalk in front of Grant's Hardware Emporium, next to the wheelbarrows. She had planted the pumpkins back in the spring, after the last frost, weeded around them during the summer, then picked them in mid-October. They were beautiful pumpkins, like fat, full moons.

Pastor Jimmy at the Harmony Worship Center ordered his flock to boycott Halloween. When his sheep began to murmur against him, he proposed they hold an end-times party instead, where the children could dress as their favorite character from the book of Revelation and get candy.

"How's that any different from Halloween?" they asked. "Why don't we just send our kids trick-or-treating, like we've always done?"

Pastor Jimmy is not fond of being second-guessed. He believes he speaks for God and people should do what he says. But he's in the wrong town for unquestioned obedience. With a scarcity of entertainment opportunities, second-guessing is a cherished pastime.

"So whadya got against trick-or-treating anyway?" they asked him.

He said it was coercive, that threatening to trick someone who doesn't give you a treat was tyranny and a poor example to the children.

"What about last Sunday when you told us if we didn't tithe, God would punish us? Wasn't that tyranny?"

Pastor Jimmy made a mental note to preach on Nadab and Abihu, who were consumed with fire after bucking the Lord. That he wasn't the Lord escaped his notice.

Sam Gardner is all for Halloween, mostly because Pastor Jimmy and Dale Hinshaw are against it. Dale believes the youth of the town are just itching to worship Satan and sacrifice a household pet or two, and Halloween is the only excuse they need.

At the October elders meeting, Dale suggested the meeting put on a haunted house in the meetinghouse basement. He wanted Sam to dress in a devil's costume, and have rats and sulfur and screaming. Maybe a fake severed limb or two. Then, when the kids were scared and crying for their mothers, they'd not let them out of the basement until they accepted Jesus as their savior.

Dale has been watching the Reverend Johnny LaCosta and taking him seriously. The week before, he'd found his cat dead on the street in front of his house and was certain devil worshipers were behind it. The cat had tire tracks on it, but Dale knew for a fact it had died from ritual torture.

Sam sat wondering why Halloween has taken such a hit. When he was growing up, Halloween was mostly about popcorn balls, throwing corn on wooden porches, and an occasional flaming bag of manure left on a grouch's doorstep. The problem, he decided, was people like Pastor Jimmy and Dale, self-appointed guardians of truth, who saw demons lurking behind every bush.

"I don't think a haunted house is a good idea," Miriam said.

"There was a time," Dale said, "when people cared about Satan infesting our youth. But if you don't care, I can't make you care. If you want to turn this town over to the Satanists, that's your business."

This was vintage Dale Hinshaw, exaggerating potential danger in order to make resistance to his ideas seem reckless and unChristian. New elders are a bit shocked the first time Dale questions their commitment to the Lord, but by the third or fourth meeting they're accustomed to it. They smile politely, thank Dale for his concern, then move on to the next agenda item, which is what they did when he suggested turning the meetinghouse basement into hell.

"Some of our teenagers have volunteered to play their guitars during meeting for worship," Judy Iverson said. "What should I tell them?"

"Sounds good to me," Sam said. He would have agreed to a drum-beating tribesman with a bone through his nose if it got Bea Majors off the organ.

It went downhill from there. Harvey Muldock proposed hanging a sign in the bathroom cautioning people not to use so much toilet paper. Fern Hampton complained that certain people weren't closing their eyes during prayer. Dale made a valiant effort to resurrect his haunted house. It was ten o'clock before Miriam could herd the ponies back to the corral, say a closing prayer, and send folks home.

The next morning at breakfast, Sam asked his boys what they wanted to be for Halloween.

"A pirate," Levi said.

"I want to be a football player," said Addison. "That means you'll have to buy me shoulder pads, a helmet, football pants and shirt, and a jock strap in case I get hit in the crunch."

Sam chuckled. "I think you mean crotch, not crunch. And I hate to burst your bubble, kiddo, but you might want to come up with a different costume."

"How about a bum with a game leg?"

"That's better," Sam agreed.

"Will you buy me crutches?"

"We can borrow a pair from Johnny Mackey at the funeral home."

The day before Halloween, they went up to the attic and rooted around in a trunk of old clothes for costumes. Sam sawed off the end of a rake handle and fashioned a peg leg for Levi the pirate. Barbara sewed him an eye patch, then taught Addison how to walk with crutches.

Sam took the boys trick-or-treating, while Barbara stayed home to pass out candy. Having lived in Harmony most of his life,

Sam knows who gives the best treats. They stopped at Opal Majors's house for popcorn balls. Arvella Miles makes caramel apples, so they visited there. Dale Hinshaw hands out Bible tracts about a little boy who was struck by a car on Halloween and died before he could ask the Lord's forgiveness for trick-or-treating, thus ensuring his eternal damnation. They skipped Dale's house.

Dale has always been more vigilant in his faith than most, but in the past couple years his religion has had an edge to it. His insurance business has been dying, and he's been looking for someone to blame. He listens to radio and television preachers and believes everything he hears. Discernment has never been Dale's strong suit. He likes easy explanations. He likes having someone else to pin his troubles on — the gays, the liberals, and the one-world-order people.

Dale's problems are his own doing. People come in for a quote on homeowners' insurance, and the next thing they know Dale is asking them if they would mind going to the Lord for a word of prayer.

"Yes, I do mind," they would like to say. "I came in here for insurance, not a revival." But they can't say that, for fear Dale will tell everyone they're atheists. Instead, they smile awkwardly and say, "Well, sure, that would be fine." The next thing they know, Dale is looming over them, urging them to their knees, beseeching the Lord to forgive their many sins.

Dale believes Satan is attacking his business because he's been praying with his customers. His response has been to pray longer and more fervently. The more he prays, the more his customers are inclined to drive to Cartersburg for their insurance needs.

It worries Sam that more people seem to be thinking like Dale. If the weather is clear, and he turns the antenna just so, he can get Channel 43 from the city. He listens to preachers tell vast arenas full of people how God wants them to be rich and how if they're sick, it's because they've sinned. The preachers are draped in gold jewelry. The only jewelry Sam has is his wedding band, which Barbara bought at Kmart on a blue-light special. Sam would like to grab those preachers by their tailored lapels and haul them to a children's hospital, so they could tell him what sin those children committed.

He can watch only about five minutes before he starts talking back to the television set. Barbara marches in and shuts it off. "Why do you watch that nonsense?" she asks. "You know it makes you mad. Why do you bother?"

"Sermon ideas," he tells her.

He's been working on a sermon in favor of Halloween, explaining how it began in the ninth century as All Hallows' Eve to honor the less-famous saints who would otherwise be forgotten, the Christians who were martyred in obscurity, perhaps burned at the stake in a small, out-of-the-way town. Sam feels a connection to them and wonders if he will likely be hounded to death in a small, out-of-the-way town.

The Sunday after Halloween, he preached about appreciating the little-known saints, like Ananias of Damascus, who restored the Apostle Paul's sight, then was never heard from again. He was a saint who did his work, then went quietly away, not expecting to be called down front during worship and given a certificate to the local Bible bookstore.

"This is the model for Christian service," Sam said in his sermon. "To labor for the Lord quietly, then move on, with no concern for honor or tribute."

There are some people Sam wished would quietly move on, though he refrained from naming names. Everyone knew he was talking about Fern Hampton, who the month before had thrown a fit when Sam inadvertently failed to call her name during Teacher Recognition Sunday. Fern had stomped out of worship. They tried to appease her by creating a special award and presenting it to her the following week, but it hadn't helped. Five weeks later, she was still pouting.

Sam has a theory: the people who talk most about being Christian are the ones least likely to act like Christians. He's been conducting an experiment during the elders meetings by observing how often each elder mentions his or her commitment to the Lord. Fern Hampton and Dale Hinshaw are running neck and neck with thirteen mentions per meeting. Miriam Hodge and Asa Peacock, who are too busy laboring for the Lord to boast about it, have gone three meetings without a mention.

After Sam gave his sermon, Dale Hinshaw stood and talked about the end-times party at the Harmony Worship Center and how twenty-three children had rebuked Satan, given their hearts to the Lord, and pledged to tithe their allowance. "I just want to say how glad I am that some churches still have a burden for the lost, and I just pray this church will return to the Lord and just plead for his gracious, tender mercy, before he hauls off and smites the whole lot of us."

Trying to follow the logic of Dale's arguments had given Sam fierce headaches —

stabbing pains between the eyes moving to a general throbbing at the back of his head. He'd gone to see Dr. Neely, who'd asked him when he had the headaches.

"Mostly during elders meetings," Sam had told him.

"Isn't Dale Hinshaw an elder at your church?"

"Yes," Sam said.

"And I suppose you've been trying to make sense out of what he says?"

"Yes," admitted Sam.

"Don't," Dr. Neely said. "It'll tax your brain. Just smile, then change the subject. Trust me on this. I've seen it before."

Sam had taken his two boys by Dr. Neely's house for Halloween. The doctor and his wife live in a small house the next block over, having sold their old home place to Sam and Barbara two years past. Some thirty years before, the Neelys' little boy, Jack, had died of leukemia. His name and height were still marked on the wall behind the curtains in Sam's dining room.

Dr. Neely had peered at Addison, momentarily confused. He looked like Jack. The dust of freckles, the short thatch of hair, the gapped-toothed grin. He'd stooped down. "And what are you supposed to be, young man?"

"A bum with a game leg."

"Oh, yes, I see. Would you like me to take a look at your leg? Maybe I can fix it. I'm a doctor, you know."

"It isn't really hurt. I'm just pretending," Addison explained.

"Oh, well, that's good to hear. I'd hate to see a little boy with a game leg."

Dr. Neely straightened up. Sam could hear his bones creak.

"How're your headaches, Sam?" he asked.

"Much better, thank you."

He dropped two Milky Ways in the boys' sacks and rubbed their heads. "You got some fine sons here, Sam. Take good care of them."

"I sure will. Boys, what do you say to Dr. Neely?"

"Thank you," they cried out.

That's why Sam liked Halloween. The slight smile of a neighbor as he leaned forward to drop Milky Ways into bags. Walking door to door with his boys — Levi and his Magic Marker pirate's stubble, Addison hobbling along on Johnny Mackey's crutches. The fat, orange moon floating just above the trees. Amanda Hodge, selling her pumpkins on a Saturday morning, earning college money so as not to be a burden. Even Ned Kivett's candy corn, aged to perfection. Even that.

Listening to Dale speak, Sam thought of Pastor Jimmy and Dale boasting how they loved the Lord, but never trusting love's power to redeem. Seeing evil where evil wasn't. In a way, Sam felt sorry for them — fear and anxiety being heavy yokes to bear.

Meanwhile, he was grateful Christmas was still two months away, that he had a brief respite before Dale went on the attack against Santa Claus. Sam could hear him now.

"Did you ever notice how Santa is spelled with the same letters as Satan? And that he wears a red suit just like Beelzebub? I tell you, people, we need to be standing firm against this. It troubles me that the rest of you have turned your faces from the truth. Here's a guy who breaks into people's houses, and you're teaching your children it's okay."

Classic Dale, looking for evil where there wasn't any. Which is why when Sam had driven past Dale's house the week before and his cat had darted out from underneath a parked car and Sam swerved but hit him anyway, he hadn't stopped to tell anyone. Who needed the trouble? Not him, that's for sure.

In addition to popcorn balls, throwing corn on wooden porches, and an occasional flaming bag of manure left on a grouch's doorstep, another Halloween staple of Sam's youth was the Great Pumpkin Toss, which began as most grand traditions do — inadvertently.

In 1927, with an excess of pumpkins, Abraham Peacock had lobbed the surplus off a fifty-foot cliff into White Lick Creek, which ran along the west edge of his farm. Around the fourth pumpkin, he spied a big rock in the creek and launched ten more pumpkins, zeroing in on the rock, until the fifteenth pumpkin hit home with a resounding splat and a burst of pumpkin innards.

The next spring he planted extra pumpkins and that fall invited his friends to join the festivities. Thus was born a hallowed tradition that continues to this day — the Great Pumpkin Toss. When Abraham Peacock died in 1943, his son, Abner, took over. Abner had a flair for promotion, and by the early sixties the Great Pumpkin Toss had grown to quite a large affair.

It was Abner Peacock who moved the toss to the Saturday after Halloween and invited the townspeople to bring their used jack-o-lanterns and contend for the hundred-dollar grand prize and the privilege of having their picture on the front page of the

Harmony Herald. Abner made his money selling pumpkins, knowing no one could toss just one pumpkin, that pumpkin tossing was addictive. He set up a pumpkin stand and sold enough to buy braces for his son, Asa, whose buckteeth were so bad he used them to open pop bottles.

In the years after the war, the toss was a fixture in Harmony, with fathers passing on pumpkin-tossing secrets to their sons — the horseshoe pitch with the half twist, the bowling-ball lob with the vertical spin, and the rare two-handed push with the fading curve. The old men down at the Coffee Cup still talk in reverent tones about 1965, the year Melvin Whicker hit the rock three times in a row with an aerodynamic, hybrid pumpkin he had developed just for the toss.

In the mid-sixties, there was also a pumpkin-stacking contest, which was discontinued after a tower of pumpkins collapsed on Abner Peacock's rat terrier, Squeaky, who never fully recovered and spent the rest of his shortened life quivering under their kitchen table, crippled by pumpkin flashbacks.

In the early seventies, the Great Pumpkin Toss fell on hard times after being rained out two years in a row. The creek was up, the rock was covered with water, Abner Peacock was in failing health, and his son, Asa, was trying to keep the farm going. In 1974, Abner died, and Asa turned the toss over to the Odd Fellows Lodge, who lacked Abner's gift for promotion.

It was Bob Miles who noticed the seventy-fifth anniversary of the Great Pumpkin Toss was fast approaching and wrote an article about it for the *Herald*. He recalled the crowds of people who'd attended the toss in his childhood and lamented its decline. He had heard the Odd Fellows were thinking of putting the toss to rest and hoped to prod them into action with an editorial accusing them of cultural apathy.

He waxed eloquent about the cherished traditions that bind people together — Thanksgiving dinners, family reunions, and pumpkin tosses — and how if these customs were neglected, society fell into decline, and before long people were setting old people out on the curb to die. The lodge responded by telling Bob if preserving the toss was crucial to Western civilization, he should donate free advertising space in the *Herald* so they could get word out.

Bob wasn't that concerned; he was just fond of hyperbole and tired of writing about town board meetings and church socials. But he did write another editorial encouraging people who wanted to preserve their way of life to join him for the seventy-fifth anniversary of the Great Pumpkin Toss.

Meanwhile, the lodge held a special meeting to discuss ways of attracting more people to the toss. They finally decided it might help to have a celebrity throw out the first pumpkin.

"The baseball teams have the president do it. Why don't we see if he's available?" Harvey Muldock suggested.

"You're crazy," said Kyle Weathers. "You think the Secret Service is gonna let the president anywhere near a bunch of people tossing pumpkins. All it'd take is one pumpkin upside the noodle and he'd be a goner. Use your head, for crying out loud."

They finally settled on Nora Nagle, the 1975 State Sausage Queen and current cashier at Kivett's Five and Dime. A few of the men suggested she wear her bathing suit, but it was pointed out that November weather was not always conducive to swimwear, so they asked her to wear her Sausage Queen sash instead, which she agreed to do.

Seeing Nora Nagle in her bathing suit has become an obsession for the men in the lodge. They have set up a phone tree to call one another when Nora goes swimming at the town pool. Within ten minutes, fifty-three Odd Fellows are congregated around the pool, plucking stray weeds from the cracks in the cement or inspecting the fence for possible security breaches.

Down at the school, they held a convocation for the children in which Asa Peacock recited the stirring history of the Great Pumpkin Toss. Then Kyle Weathers raised the stakes by donating a year's worth of free haircuts to the winner of the toss. Uly Grant at the hardware store upped the ante with a five-gallon bucket of driveway sealant. Over at the Coffee Cup, bets were placed, with the odds favoring Howard Whicker, Melvin Whicker's son, with his aerodynamic, hybrid pumpkins.

The morning of the toss dawned damp and cold. At ten o'clock, the rain stopped and the sun came out. By eleven, it was perfect weather for pumpkin tossing. The pumpkins were wiped dry to avoid a repeat of the 1959 disaster when Murray Newlin, using a bowling-ball lob with a vertical spin, had the pumpkin slip from his hand on the backswing and clobber Robert Miles, Sr., smack on the head. It jarred something loose. His IQ slipped south thirty points, and shortly afterward he joined the John Birch Society.

The water in the creek was down, and a large portion of the rock was exposed. "It'll be great tossing today," Asa Peacock said. "Like aiming at a barn."

At eleven o'clock, Sam Gardner gave the blessing of the pumpkins, and then Asa Peacock cut the ribbon with a pair of hedge clippers to begin the festivities. There were shouts and applause and a scattering of wolf whistles as Nora Nagle, wearing her Sausage Queen sash, stepped forward to toss the ceremonial pumpkin.

"She don't look strong enough to even pick that pumpkin up," Kyle Weathers whispered to Asa.

Nora grasped the pumpkin with both hands and, lifting it a few inches off the ground, waddled it over to the edge of the cliff. She gave a brief speech, recalling the honor of being selected the State Sausage Queen in 1975, but that tossing the first pumpkin on the seventy-fifth anniversary of the Great Pumpkin Toss was an even higher privilege. Bob Miles snapped her picture. Then she bent down, grasped the pumpkin, rocked back and forth three times, and launched the pumpkin.

It flew in an arc out from the cliff, spinning on its axis.

"Well, I'll be," Kyle Weathers said.

"That's a two-handed push with a fading curve. I haven't seen that since Melvin Whicker threw it in '65. I wonder where she learned it?"

The pumpkin hung in the air, then hurtled toward the left of the rock. Nora twisted her hips, willing it to move right, which it did, hitting the rock dead center with a tremendous slap.

No one had ever hit the center of the rock. Not even Melvin Whicker, with his aerodynamic, hybrid pumpkins. Up until now, they had all been glancing blows. Now, Nora Nagle, on her very first toss, had hit the bull's-eye.

The Odd Fellows stood speechless. Bob Miles leaned over the cliff and snapped a picture.

The pressure was on, and the tossing began in earnest. But it was as if an invisible shield now protected the rock. Ten pumpkins, then twenty and fifty and a hundred pumpkins, lay broken in the creek. The rock seemed to taunt them, daring them to hit it.

By noontime, all the pumpkins had been tossed.

Eighty-five men stood looking over the cliff, dejected.

"Looks like we didn't have a winner,"

Kyle Weathers said. "I guess that means we'll have a bigger pot for next year."

Sam Gardner said, "What do you mean? Nora hit the rock. She's the winner."

"That was a ceremonial throw," Kyle protested. "That wasn't a real toss. It don't count."

He probably could have gotten away with it, except that it was the seventy-fifth anniversary and the men had brought their wives, all of whom began to boo Kyle.

In the end, the Odd Fellows awarded Nora the hundred dollars.

"What about the free haircuts for a year and the driveway sealant?" asked Jessie Peacock. "What about that?"

"Yeah, what about that?" Sam said.

"Traitor," Kyle hissed at Sam.

Nora wasn't all that keen about Kyle cutting her hair. She had serious reservations about sporting a flattop haircut with whitewalls. She gave the coupon to Sam.

Uly Grant lifted the bucket of driveway sealant and handed it to Nora. Her driveway was gravel, but she didn't want to appear ungrateful, so she smiled at Uly and thanked him. Then she gave a little speech about what an honor it was to win the seventy-fifth annual Great Pumpkin Toss, and how she hadn't even really tried, which made it all the worse for the Odd Fellows, because it implied that beating them required no special effort.

After her speech, the Odd Fellows retreated to their lodge to lick their wounds. "A woman," they grumbled. "Can you believe that? What is this world coming to?"

Kyle looked at Asa Peacock. "You oughta be ashamed of yourself."

"What'd I do?"

"It was your idea to have her toss the first pumpkin. I hope you're happy."

"I thought it was Vinny's idea," Asa said.

"Don't pin it on me," Vinny objected. "I wasn't even at that meeting. I heard it was Harvey's idea."

"Not me, mister, I wanted the president."

They went round and round, each of the men blaming someone else. It was not their finest hour.

Back at the cliff, Nora Nagle and the other women were savoring their victory.

"Did you see the look on their faces when you hit that rock?" Jessie Peacock said. "It was priceless." She peered over the cliff at the rock. "How'd you hit that all the way from here?"

Nora chuckled. "Amanda Hodge gave me the pumpkins she had left over from Halloween, and I practiced tossing them from the Hodges' hayloft. Miriam taught me. Did you know her father was Melvin Whicker? Well, anyway, he taught her, and she taught me. The two-handed push with a fading curve."

"I wouldn't let that out if I were you," Jessie advised. "I'm not sure the men could bear to hear it. They're awful fragile."

Thus, one secret piles upon another, breeding mistrust and cynicism. Your cat is found dead in the street, but no one's knocked on your door to confess. Maybe it was an accident, but probably not. Probably it was Satan worshipers. Classified pumpkin-tossing information is passed on to a select few members of a pumpkin-tossing cartel whose goal is nothing less than the overthrow of the Odd Fellows Lodge.

"She set us up," Kyle Weathers said, back at the lodge. "Now that I think about it, we didn't even ask her to throw out the first pumpkin. She came to us. It was her idea."

That must have been it. What else could explain it? What were the chances a rookie pumpkin tosser, a woman at that, could hit the rock?

"I wouldn't put it past her," Ernie Matthews said. "I heard her uncle was one of the judges that picked her as the Sausage

Queen back in '75. I've always said those Nagles were a shady bunch."

"That ain't the worst of it," Dale Hinshaw said. "Last week, I seen her drive past my house real slow, and the next day my cat turned up dead. Now if that ain't suspicious, I don't know what is."

"I tell you one thing," Kyle Weathers said, "that woman bears watching. She was gone all those years. Lord knows what she coulda been up to. I say we keep a close eye on her."

"I'll watch her at the pool," Ernie Matthews volunteered.

"I'll help you," Kyle said.

"You can count on me," Harvey pledged.

It had been a long day and the Odd Fellows were tired from tossing pumpkins, though even in their weariness they would stay awake and aware, diligence being the price to be paid if Western civilization is to be preserved.

Sixteen
Thanksgiving

It was Sam's idea for Barbara to help the Friendly Women's Circle make noodles the Tuesday before Thanksgiving. She doesn't do much in the way of fellowship, doesn't hold teas for the ladies, teach a women's Bible study, or serve on committees just because there's a vacancy. She believes having to put up with Sam griping about the church is obligation enough.

So when he suggested she help the Circle make noodles, she said, "If you think it's such a good idea, why don't you do it?"

"That's the very thing I mean," he said. "You're too cynical. Maybe spending more time with fellow Christians would help your Christian walk."

"My Christian walk is fine, thank you."

Barbara has never been the typical minister's wife. She likes a salty joke now and then and reads novels that would not receive the Friendly Woman seal of approval —

books about women who have given themselves over to indiscriminate romance and don't appear to feel sorry about it.

Sam bought her a Christian novel, which was also filled with indiscriminate romance, though by the book's end the women had repented of their sins, joined the church, and were working at the church rummage sale to the glory of God the Father.

When Sam had first talked about becoming a pastor, she went along with it, thinking he'd get over it in a few years, then become a schoolteacher or insurance salesman. She hadn't braced herself for the long haul. It annoys her when people invoke Jesus' name at the drop of a hat, which means she's irritated most of the time. Dolores Hinshaw tells how she forgot to add the garlic powder to her sausage cheeseballs, but, praise Jesus, they turned out just fine. Barbara has a sneaking suspicion that with all the other problems in the world, Jesus doesn't give a flying fig about Dolores Hinshaw's cheeseballs, though being the minister's wife, she can't say that. Instead, she smiles and says, "Well, isn't that precious."

But Barbara drew the line at noodle making. She told Sam, "Your call to the ministry was not two for the price of one. If you think noodle making is a Christian virtue, you are free to make noodles. Just don't volunteer me." Which he forgot all about when Fern Hampton stopped by his office the week before Thanksgiving to gripe that the Circle had fallen behind in their noodle production.

"We're ten quarts short of where we should be this time of year. You're the pastor. What are you going to do about it?" she demanded.

"I don't know," he said. "Maybe Barbara could help."

"We'll just count on it," Fern said, then stood and marched from his office.

Sam went home for lunch. After lunch he gathered the dirty dishes from the table, carried them over to the sink, and began washing them. That's when Barbara knew something was up.

"Why are you being so helpful?" she asked.

"Oh, no special reason. I've just been thinking how hard you work around here, and that I've not been good about thanking you."

"Okay, Sam, what's her name, and how long have you been seeing her?"

"What are you talking about?"

"Sam Gardner, I've known you eighteen years. You've done something wrong and now you feel guilty. What'd you do?"

Sam winced. "It'll only take a couple hours of your time."

Barbara groaned. "What did you volunteer me for this time?"

"Helping the Friendly Women make noodles next Tuesday."

"The week of Thanksgiving! Sam, we're having all your family over for dinner and you volunteered me to make noodles? What in the world were you thinking? That was my day to clean the house."

"I can clean the house."

"Hah!"

Sam's idea of housecleaning was to swipe a rag across the coffee table, stuff the clutter under the couch, and then light a candle to make the house smell nice.

Barbara doesn't get mad often, but she did then. Since the children weren't there, she lit into Sam, complaining about how keeping the family going was hard enough, and now Sam wanted her to keep the Friendly Women afloat, too, and how she was only one person and couldn't do it all, and why did they have to make all those stupid noodles anyway when they could buy them for next to nothing, and how come Sam jumped every time Fern Hampton snapped her fingers.

When she paused to breathe, Sam fled out

the back door and holed up in his office working on his sermon. He'd written a message on the blessings of family, but was now thinking of preaching a sermon endorsing the Apostle Paul's advice to remain single.

Sam waited until the kids returned from school before going back home. Barbara had settled down by then and was feeling ashamed for the way she'd yelled at him. Besides, she'd told herself, it wasn't like the Circle was making the noodles to line their own pockets. All their money went to Brother Norman's shoe ministry to the Choctaw Indians. And here she was, with six pairs of shoes, while shoeless Choctaw children were stepping on nails and dying of tetanus.

She apologized to Sam and told him she'd be happy to help the Friendly Women. "Just don't volunteer me," she said. "If something needs to be done, don't just assume I'll do it. Ask me first, instead of telling me."

"I don't know why I do that," Sam said. "It's just that Fern was staring me down. I tell you, Barbara, you don't know what it's like to be stared down by a Friendly Woman. I felt lucky to escape with my life."

That was Friday. The next Tuesday, Barbara woke up early, got the boys out the door to school, cleaned the kitchen, and was down at the meetinghouse by nine o'clock to make noodles. Fern was there, barking orders to the flock of Friendly Women.

They floured down the noodle table and began rolling out dough. They talked about Thanksgiving and who was going where and what they were serving. Dolores Hinshaw mentioned how she'd misplaced her mother's turkey Jell-O recipe. "I was just so upset, so I took it to the Lord and asked him to show me where the recipe was. And he told me to go to his Word, and there it was, smack in between First and Second Chronicles. It just isn't Thanksgiving without turkey Jell-O."

"It sounds scrumptious," Barbara said, struggling mightily to control her gag reflex.

"I'll make you some, if you'd like," Dolores offered.

"That's very kind of you, Dolores, but I wouldn't want you to go to all that trouble."

"It's no trouble at all," Dolores said. "I'll have Dale bring it by Thanksgiving Day."

That will certainly thrill Sam, Barbara thought. Dale Hinshaw dropping by their house on Thanksgiving. Helping himself to a chair at the kitchen table, making himself at home, ignoring hints that it was time he left. Dale would offer to say a prayer, in which he would thank the good Lord for his mercy in these last days. "Lord, we just know you're fed up with all this liberal gobbledygook, and we just thank you for your patience in not coming back and just killing the whole lot of us."

Oh, well, that's what Sam got for volunteering her to make noodles.

"Where are you going for Thanksgiving, Fern?" Barbara asked.

Fern was quiet for a moment, then said, "Oh, nowhere special. I was just gonna stay home and watch the Macy's parade."

"I thought you had some family over in Cartersburg."

"That was my sister Frieda, but she's passed away."

"What about your nephew Ervin? Why don't you spend it with him?" Miriam asked.

"He went to Cleveland to a manhole cover convention and is staying over a few days to see the sights."

The Friendly Women glanced at one another, the weight of Christian guilt lying heavily upon them. They knew they should invite Fern to join them for Thanksgiving, but they each hesitated, hoping someone else would take up that cross.

"I'd be happy to have you come to my house," Opal Majors said, "but I've already got two card tables set up in the living room and four people on the couch. I don't know where I'd put you." She smiled pleasantly at Barbara. "How are you and Sam enjoying your home? You have such a lovely place. I just love what you've done with your dining room. It's so spacious. The Lord has certainly blessed you with a beautiful home, that's for sure."

"If I had a dining room like yours, I'd have guests every day," Bea Majors said.

Barbara was cornered. The Friendly Women were staring at her expectantly. There was no escaping. They continued to stare. Finally, she broke. "Fern, we'd be happy to have you join us for Thanksgiving," she said, then held her breath, praying Fern would decline her offer.

"Why, thank you, Barbara. I'd be happy to."

The other Friendly Women sighed in relief, grateful to have dodged the Fern Hampton bullet.

Barbara wasn't sure the best way to tell Sam what she'd done. That evening, she made his favorite dessert, bread pudding. When it came time to put the boys to bed, she told Sam to relax, that he'd worked hard that day and deserved a break. She tucked the boys in, then brought him a serving of bread pudding. He looked at her warily.

"Any certain reason you made bread pudding?"

"Oh, no special reason. I just want to pamper you a little bit, that's all." She sat down beside him and snuggled in. "How about we go to bed a little early tonight, honey."

"Not till you've told me what you're up to. You've done something you know I won't like. I can tell. What'd you do?"

"Now, Sam, it's only for one day, and it won't hurt a thing. Besides, when it's all over, you'll be glad we did it."

"Glad we did what?"

"Glad we invited Fern Hampton to Thanksgiving dinner," Barbara said, wincing.

"We did what?!"

"Sam, she didn't have anyplace else to go, and all the women were staring at me waiting for me to invite her."

Sam groaned. "I can't believe you invited Fern Hampton to our house for Thanksgiving."

"You're the one who told me I was too cynical, that I needed to spend more time with church people and improve my Christian walk. Make up your mind, Sam. Do you want me to spend more time with the church members or not?"

"Fern Hampton for Thanksgiving dinner is not what I had in mind," he said.

"Then you should have been more specific."

Sam sighed.

Fern was the first to show on Thanksgiving morning. Sam and Barbara were lying in bed when the doorbell sounded a little after seven. They heard the door open, then listened as Fern rustled around downstairs.

"Yoo-hoo," she called out. "Is anyone home? I'm here."

"We're upstairs, Fern," Sam yelled. "We'll be right down."

They put on their robes and went downstairs. Fern was standing in their kitchen. "I thought I'd get here early and help with the turkey," she said. She began rummaging through the cabinets. "Where do you keep your roasting pan?"

Barbara leaned toward Sam. "This is all your fault," she hissed in his ear. She took Fern by the elbow. "Fern, you needn't bother. You're our guest. You go visit with Sam." She turned toward Sam. "Sam, why don't you show Fern to the living room, and you can visit in there."

But Fern wouldn't hear of it. She kept searching through the cabinets. "Ah, ha! Here's the roaster!" Sam and Barbara had planned on deep-frying the turkey. The week before, they'd bought a turkey fryer at Grant's Hardware. They tried explaining that to Fern, to no avail. "Frying a turkey? Whoever heard of such foolishness?" she said. "It's a good thing I showed up when I did, or this day would have been a flop."

From that moment on, Barbara was banished to the sidelines. She'd start to do something and Fern would take over. "Now, honey, why not let's put a little more milk in those potatoes. We wouldn't want them lumpy, would we? No oysters in your dressing? I think I might have a can at home. Why don't you be a dear and run and fetch them."

The others arrived a little before noon — Sam's mom and dad, and his bachelor brother, Roger, from the city. Fern directed them where to sit, then took the chair at the head of the table, and asked Sam to pray. The doorbell rang just as they lowered their heads.

"Excuse me," Sam said. "Let me get that, and I'll be right back."

He opened the front door, and there was Dale Hinshaw, holding what appeared to be beige Jell-O. "I'm here with your turkey Jell-O," he said. "The missus just finished it." He peered around Sam and into the dining room. "Is that Fern in there? Hey, Fern."

"Hi, Dale. Come on in."

"Don't mind if I do. Say, it sure smells sure good in here."

"It's the turkey," Fern said. "They were gonna fry it in grease, but I got here just in time to stop them."

Sam stepped forward. "Thank you for the Jell-O, Dale. It was very thoughtful of you. Please thank your wife for us. Well, we were just sitting down to dinner, so we won't keep you. I'm sure you want to get home to your family."

"Nope. The kids aren't coming till tomorrow."

"Why don't you stay and eat with us," Fern said. "There's plenty of food. Sam and Barbara won't mind."

"I'm sure Dale probably has other plans, and we wouldn't want to put him out," Sam said, putting a hand on Dale's back to steer him toward the door.

"Well, thank you, Fern. I think I will stay," Dale said. "Say, why don't I phone the missus and get her over here, too. Where's your phone, Sam?"

Sam nodded glumly toward the kitchen.

They could hear Dale through the kitchen door. "No, they don't mind. They begged

243

me to stay. I think they're lonely. Sure, we can wait."

He sat back down at the table. "She'll be here quick as a wink. She wanted to take a bath first, and do her hair."

"Why don't I put the food back on the stove, so it doesn't get cold," Barbara said, rising to her feet.

"I'll help," said Sam.

She cornered him in the kitchen. "Well, Sam, it looks like you got your wish. I'm spending more time with the church members. Have you noticed any improvement in my Christian walk?"

Two hours later, Dale's wife showed. The potatoes had set up like cement, the gravy was skinned over, and the turkey had turned a pale gray.

Their table sat eight people, nine in a pinch. With Dolores Hinshaw, there were now ten.

"Sam can sit on the couch," Fern said. "He doesn't mind."

Dale cleared his throat. "Why don't we go to the Lord for a word of prayer. Lord, first off, we just thank you for your love today, for not just grabbing us by the neck and kickin' our heinies like we deserve. Lord, our hearts are burdened thinking of everyone who don't know you — the Muslims, the Catholics, the Chinese. We just pray they accept your truth, so's you won't have to kill 'em. Thank you for this food and that Fern showed up in time to save the turkey. Amen. Say, Fern, could you pass the dressing down this way."

"Help yourself," Fern said. "Those are real oysters in that dressing. I put 'em in there myself. Barbara wasn't gonna put any in."

Barbara smiled weakly. "I wasn't sure if everyone liked oysters," she explained.

"Well, of course everyone likes oysters," Fern said. "What's not to like?"

Sam's younger child, Addison, looked at Sam. "Daddy, what did Dale Hinshaw say about the Chinese?"

"I'll explain it later," Sam said. "Right now, we're eating."

"Just praying they'll know the Lord, that's all," Dale said cheerfully. "Here you go, Sam. Help yourself to some of this turkey Jell-O. Now don't chip your tooth on a bone. The missus tries to get most of them out, but you never know."

Sam spent the rest of the meal thinking what might have happened if he'd accepted the job at that rich church in North Carolina the year before. He'd probably be eating Thanksgiving dinner in a country club, then maybe smoking a Cuban cigar and drinking a snifter of brandy. His wife wouldn't be mad at him. He looked up to see Dale Hinshaw give a slight belch, then reach in his shirt pocket and pull out a toothpick, on which he commenced to chew.

After dinner, they retired to the living room to watch the parades and the football games. Fern sat in Sam's recliner and Dale stretched out on the couch, while Sam and Barbara served pumpkin pie.

"Say, you wouldn't have some ice cream to go on top of this, would you?" Dale asked.

"No, we don't," Sam said. "I'm sorry."

Dale frowned. "It's just not the same without ice cream."

"Sam, I have ice cream at my house. Why don't you be a dear and run and get it," Fern suggested.

Dale looked at Sam expectantly.

It was eight o'clock before everyone left, and ten o'clock before Sam and Barbara got the boys in bed, cleaned the kitchen, and then collapsed on the couch, where they lay perfectly still. Sam didn't speak, fearing the wrong word spoken in haste would do irreparable harm to his marriage.

The phone rang. Sam groaned, struggled to his feet, and walked into the kitchen.

"Hello."

"Hi, Sam. It's me, Fern."

He could hear Fern speak to someone else. "I told you they'd still be up."

"Ervin just got in from his manhole cover convention and he's nearly starved. I'm sending him your way for some leftovers."

"Gee, Fern, I'm sorry, but I just fed all the leftovers to the dog." Then he hung up the phone and sat back down on the couch.

"We don't have a dog," Barbara said.

"I know."

"I guess this proves your theory wrong."

"What theory?"

"That spending time with church members improves your Christian walk. They've not been gone an hour and you're already lying like a rug."

Sam didn't say anything for several minutes. Then he said, "I don't suppose it matters to you that the Apostle Paul advised women to be submissive to their husbands."

"Which might explain why he was never able to find a wife," she observed.

They lay on the couch. The house was dark except for a faint glow in the kitchen from the light over the sink.

"I suppose we ought to go to bed," Sam said. They heaved themselves off the couch and trudged up the stairs. They didn't even bother to wash. They just fell into bed, where Sam fell promptly to sleep. But Barbara lay awake, pondering why the things that made a person a better Christian were always so irritating. She wondered how she could even tell if she were a better Christian. Probably when people no longer irritated her, she thought. If that were the case, she had a long way to go.

Seventeen
A Christmas Revelation

With the holidays looming, people's thoughts have turned to Deena Morrison, who is still unattached. Christmas is a sad time to be alone, and everyone was hoping she'd be married by now. Back in March, at the Easter service, she'd sat with Sam's brother, Roger, which had buoyed the town's spirits. But Roger couldn't believe someone so beautiful would be interested in him, so he never phoned her. Though he thinks about her. And she thinks about him and wonders why he doesn't call.

Meanwhile, certain people have been trying to fix her up with their unattached relatives. Oscar and Livinia Purdy, of the Dairy Queen Purdys, have been dropping hints that their son Myron is available and will one day inherit the Dairy Queen. He drives an immense four-wheel-drive pickup truck with a personalized license plate that reads *2HOT*, which tells you everything you need to know about Myron Purdy. He's asked Deena out three times, but she can't get past that license plate.

She's decided to stop trying to find a man, that if it's meant to be, it'll just happen. It's a rather fatalistic view and contrary to her usual approach, which is to set a goal and work toward it. But she's been working toward a husband for three years with no discernible progress, so she's open to a new approach.

The Friendly Women's Circle has not given up their sacred obligation to see her wed. Unbeknownst to her, they wrote letters to their fellow Friendly Women in other Quaker meetings asking for snapshots and biographies of the unattached men in their congregations, which they presented to Deena one Sunday after meeting for worship.

"Think of it as an early Christmas present," they told her.

Deena was not happy with the thought of being peddled across the state at various churches, but she took the pictures anyway so as not to hurt their feelings. She thumbed through them when she got home, and it soon became apparent why these men were unattached.

"He's not so bad," her grandmother

Mabel said, pointing to a picture. "I wonder why he shaved his head?"

"He's probably a member of a gang."

"Yul Brynner was bald. Women were nuts about him."

"Yes, I suppose so," Deena admitted. "But look at his left eye, how it drifts to the side."

Mabel studied the photograph. "I think it makes him look mysterious."

"I don't like mysterious," Deena said. "Mysterious men always have something to hide. Like a body in their crawl space or a wife in another state."

Mabel mused over another picture. "This man says he likes to travel internationally."

"That probably means he spends his vacation fishing in Canada. Look at his shirt. It says *On The Seventh Day, God Fished*. No, thank you."

"Your grandfather liked to fish, and he was a nice man."

"I have no problems with men fishing. I just don't want to date a man who wears T-shirts about fishing."

The pictures were bad enough, but what really steamed Deena was when the December edition of the church newsletter landed in her mailbox with her name in the Friendly Women's column. *Please pray for Deena as she tries to find a man.*

She wonders if moving to the city would increase her chances for matrimony. She'd confided in Sam that she was thinking of leaving. He hated the thought of it, since she helped offset the Dale Effect. Whenever they had visitors, he steered them toward Deena, so Harmony Friends would appear more enlightened and progressive than it was. With Deena gone, he'd have to introduce them to Dale, which would have a chilling effect.

Deena reads books written by people no one has ever heard of, books Miss Rudy at the library has to order in special. She can talk with visitors on a variety of subjects, from the conflict in the Middle East to gardening. Dale reads the *End Times* newsletter by Brother Eddie from Sheboygan, Wisconsin, and asks visitors if they think Jesus will return before or after the Great Tribulation.

Sam did what he always does when he fears someone might leave the church — he asked her to serve on a committee so she'd feel obligated to stay. Specifically, the Peace and Social Concerns Committee, whose bloom had faded under the leadership of Dolores Hinshaw. Dolores's response to staggering human suffering was to launch salvation balloons with her husband, Dale.

Sam eased Dolores out of the picture by forming a new committee and putting her in charge of it — the Harmony Friends Bicentennial Celebration Committee — which would begin planning now for their two-hundredth anniversary in 2026. Sam was relatively certain he'd be gone by then.

With Dolores out of the way, he nominated Deena to take her place as head of the Peace and Social Concerns Committee, and in she went.

"How long is my term?" she asked Sam, after accepting the position.

"Deena, with this committee we don't tend to think in terms of years. Can a job really ever be finished as long as even one person anywhere is suffering?"

That's when she knew she'd been hoodwinked.

"You know, Deena," Sam continued, "it's been so long since we've heard from the Peace and Social Concerns Committee, maybe you should bring the message the Sunday before Christmas. It's our biggest Sunday. Everyone's here. You'll have a captive audience."

After eighteen Christmas sermons, Sam had run out of things to say. He'd never liked that Sunday anyway, with the twice-a-year attenders arriving late and clomping down front to the empty seats, distracting everyone else.

The prospect of delivering a message to the congregation intrigued Deena. She called a meeting of the committee, their first meeting in two years, and asked for sermon ideas. They were singularly unhelpful, except to suggest she avoid two topics — peace and social concerns.

"Dale Hinshaw doesn't like it when we talk about peace," Ellis Hodge said. "He believes peace won't come until Jesus returns and that people who work for peace are opposing God's plan, so I'd avoid that subject if I were you."

"And try not to say anything that'll make the Republicans mad," Bill Muldock suggested. "None of that helping-the-poor stuff."

"If people get mad when we talk about peace and social concerns, why do we have a Peace and Social Concerns Committee?" Deena asked.

"Because we've always had one," they said.

Word of Deena's new job spread through the meeting quickly. The Friendly Women were not at all pleased. "If I've seen it once, I've seen a hundred times," Bea Majors said. "These do-gooder types get caught up in some liberal cause, and then they stop shaving their legs. The next thing you know, they've moved to California, joined some cult, and changed their name to Moonflower. We need to get her a man, before she's ruined."

Fern Hampton peered at Eunice Muldock. "Isn't your son Johnny coming home for Christmas?"

"His name is Jimmy," Eunice corrected her. "And, yes, he'll be home this Friday."

"Why don't you invite Deena over for supper and let 'em look each other over," Fern suggested. "It couldn't hurt."

"I don't know. I don't think Deena is his type."

Fern snorted. "Well, of course she's his type. She's a woman, he's a man. What other types are there?"

Another type is gay, which is what Jimmy is, though Eunice didn't want to mention that, so she kept quiet.

Fern mistook her silence for agreement. "Now don't hover over them," she said. "He can't propose if you and Harvey are hanging around like a couple of old geezers. Eat dinner, then excuse yourselves and go for a drive. Give love room to weave its magic."

That these arrangements were made without the consent of Deena and Jimmy didn't seem to trouble the Friendly Women, who asked Eunice to report on her progress at their January meeting.

As for Deena, when Eunice invited her over for dinner, she was mildly interested. Jimmy was college-educated and artistic, and he lived in Chicago.

"He doesn't wear fishing T-shirts, does he?" she asked Eunice.

"No, he doesn't like to fish."

When Deena heard that, she decided to buy a new dress.

Jimmy was a harder sell. When his mother mentioned a friend of hers was dropping by, he immediately grew suspicious.

"Which friend? Fern? Bea?"

"No, her name is Deena. I don't think you've ever met her. She owns the coffee shop here in town."

"Mom, you're not fixing me up, are you?"

"Oh, don't be silly. I wouldn't do that. I just thought you'd enjoy meeting her. Stop being so suspicious."

Jimmy had decided before coming home that this would be the trip he'd tell his father, Harvey, he was gay. Even though he suspected his dad already knew, to have it confirmed would be painful, on account of he was his father's only son. The Muldock legacy would end with Jimmy. Even worse, there'd be no Muldock heir to inherit Harvey's Cranbrook convertible.

Harvey blamed his wife. He'd read that homosexuality was caused by a shortage of testosterone during the development of the fetus. He'd thought about asking Eunice why she hadn't made more testosterone, but didn't want to start a fight. The last time they'd argued, he'd had to cook his own meals for a week.

Jimmy arrived in town late Friday night. He woke up Saturday morning and went to the Coffee Cup with Harvey. He'd hoped to tell his father over a leisurely breakfast, but the Coffee Cup didn't seem like the place to do it. It didn't feel right talking to his father about such things with Asa Peacock in the next booth cracking jokes.

"Yeah," Asa was saying, "I was milking the cow this morning, and this bug started buzzing around the cow's head and flew right in her ear. Next thing I know, the bug squirted out in my bucket. Yep, went in one ear and out the udder."

This was not an environment conducive to personal disclosure, so Jimmy kept quiet.

Deena spent the day working on a social-concerns sermon that wouldn't offend Dale Hinshaw or make her sound too much like a Democrat, which was not an easy balance to strike. She decided in the end to warn against urban sprawl and leave it at that. That was a safe topic in a town that hasn't had a new house built in twenty years.

She had hoped to be more prophetic, to use the sermon as an opportunity to challenge indifference to human suffering. But it's not an easy thing to confront people you love, so she went with urban sprawl, though was ashamed of her cowardice.

She finished the sermon, took a bath, put on her new dress, and arrived at the Muldocks' just as Eunice was pulling the pot roast from the oven. Jimmy was a pleasant surprise. Deena feared he might look like Harvey — thin on top with tufts of hair over his ears, leaning toward portly, and wearing a baseball cap. But he wasn't like that at all. *Chiseled* was the word that came to mind.

It took a moment for Deena to find her voice. Who had been keeping this man a secret? she wondered. What a dreamboat! Blue eyes, thick black hair. He looked like John Kennedy, Jr. She suddenly felt the need to sit down.

Dinner was a blur. The pot roast was tougher than asphalt, but she scarcely noticed. Her knee accidentally brushed against his under the table. He looked up and smiled. She blushed.

Eunice and Harvey began clearing the table, and then Eunice turned to Harvey and said, "I need to go to Cartersburg to buy a few more Christmas presents. Let's go."

"Why do I have to go?" Harvey asked. "I want to stay here and visit with Deena."

"Stop arguing and get your coat on."

They left, and there sat Deena and Jimmy, smiling at each other.

"I understand you own your own business," Jimmy said.

"Yes, I own the coffee shop here in town."

They discussed coffee for a few moments. "So, are you married?" Jimmy asked after a while. "Do you have a family?"

"No, I'm single." She hesitated, "And how about you? You're single, too, aren't you?"

"Actually, no, I'm involved with someone."

Deena felt the joy drain out of her. Of course, he would be involved with someone, she thought. He's the first interesting man I've met in nine months. Of course, he would be spoken for. She tried to appear unperturbed. "Tell me about your friend. What's her name?"

"Dan," Jimmy said. "She's a he. I'm gay."

Deena reddened. "I'm sorry. I didn't

know. I thought when your mother invited me over that you were unattached."

"I'm sorry she gave you that impression. My mom keeps thinking if I meet the right woman, I won't be gay anymore. I must say she has good taste. You're a beautiful woman. I love your dress."

"You do? You don't think it makes me look fat?"

"Not at all. It complements you perfectly."

"Thank you, that's kind of you to say."

There was an awkward pause. "I've never really talked with a gay person before," Deena said.

Jimmy chuckled. "I'll bet you have. You just didn't know they were gay. It's not something most of us go around talking about."

"I suppose you have a point," Deena said. "Do your parents know?"

"Mom does, but not Dad. At least we've never talked about it. I was going to raise the subject this weekend."

"I'm curious why you would even bring it up," Deena said.

"I want them to meet Dan. If you had been with someone for eight years, wouldn't you want your parents to meet him?"

Deena thought for a moment. "Of course. I hadn't thought of it in those terms."

"Don't feel bad. A lot of people haven't."

"That's a shame," Deena said. "Maybe if we just talked honestly about it, we wouldn't be so afraid of it." She paused. "You know, Jimmy, the church put me in charge of our Peace and Social Concerns Committee. I have to bring the message tomorrow. Maybe I should talk about how we treat gay people."

"I would avoid that topic if I were you," Jimmy counseled. "It tends to upset people."

"I don't think it would these people," Deena said. "They're good people. They have their oddities, but down deep they're nice people."

So the next morning she rose early, wrote another sermon, put on her new dress, and walked the three blocks to the meeting-house. It was packed. She looked around for an empty seat. Then Sam noticed her and motioned for her to come sit with him behind the pulpit. They sang, took up the offering, and prayed for the Christmas travelers and those without family.

Then Deena stood to preach. She mentioned she'd been placed in charge of the Peace and Social Concerns Committee and that Sam had asked her to bring today's message. People shifted in their seats. This was an intriguing change — a sermon from someone who'd never preached before. And Deena Morrison at that, a veritable feast for the eyes.

In keeping with the holidays, she talked about how Jesus had come to share the tender mercy of God with the people of Harmony Friends. All across the meeting room, people nodded in agreement. They were all for the tender mercy of God, especially when it was directed toward them. But it's not just for us, Deena added. They nodded their heads in agreement. Of course it wasn't, they thought. It was for others also. Others who were like them, for instance.

In fact, she said, God's mercy was for all people. Even people who were different. Homosexuals, for instance.

At the mention of that word, the meetinghouse grew deathly still. People leaned forward, focused and attentive. Jimmy motioned for her to cut it short, but she plunged ahead, talking about how she'd met a gay man that very week, in this very town, and how kind he was. Harvey Muldock glanced at Eunice. The other men began eyeing one another suspiciously. They reached over and put their arms around their wives.

Halfway through her talk, it occurred to

Deena that she had seriously misjudged the open-mindedness of Harmony Friends Meeting. She turned and looked at Sam, who was seated behind her, his face buried in his hands, wishing he had prepared an innocuous sermon on the birth of Jesus and the wise men and shepherds.

Afterward, Deena stood at the back door to shake hands. Most everyone left by the side door, except for Miriam Hodge, who thanked Deena for giving them something to think about.

Dale Hinshaw paused long enough to show Deena the Bible verse in Leviticus calling for the death of homosexuals.

"Oh, yes," she said. "I'm familiar with that passage. It's right before the verse that forbids dwarves and people with poor eyesight from serving as priests."

"Well, I don't know about that," Dale admitted. "I haven't read that part."

"Perhaps you should," Deena said sweetly. "It always helps to interpret biblical passages in their proper context."

This did not deter Dale from calling an emergency meeting of the elders, where, over the protests of Miriam Hodge and Sam, Deena was deposed as head of the Peace and Social Concerns Committee. The coup was startling in its swiftness, with

Dolores Hinshaw reclaiming the throne a half hour after worship, pledging to devote her considerable energies to the salvation balloons ministry.

Mabel Morrison was proud of her granddaughter and told her so. "If wise people don't start speaking up about this matter, people like Dale Hinshaw will always carry the day. I'm proud of you, honey."

"It appears I'm not destined to have a conventional life with a husband and children," Deena said, "so I might as well be a reformer."

At the Muldock house, it was very quiet. Eunice heated up the leftovers from the night before. Harvey set out the placemats while Jimmy poured the iced tea. They took their places at the kitchen table.

"You know," Harvey said, chewing thoughtfully on a piece of pot roast, which a night in the refrigerator had not improved, "that wasn't a bad sermon. It made me think. And what I think, is that if there was someone in my family who was that way, I could accept that."

That was all he said.

There was more chewing. Jimmy wiped his mouth on a napkin, then reached across the table and laid his hand on his father's arm. "Thank you, Dad."

That was all he said.

They looked over at Eunice. "Care for more pot roast?" she asked.

"No, thank you," Harvey and Jimmy said. That was all they said.

Eighteen
Dale's Crusade

Three weeks after Deena Morrison's sermon on the mercy of God, people were still buzzing about her mentioning the "H" word in public. Certain Friendly Women had been particularly distressed and were rethinking their commitment to see her wed.

"Maybe the reason she's not married is because she's, you know, that way herself," Bea Majors speculated at their weekly gathering.

"It wouldn't surprise me in the least," Fern Hampton said. "My nephew Ervin was hers for the asking, but do you think she was interested? Not for a minute."

"What more proof do we need?" Dolores Hinshaw asked.

"Maybe Ervin wasn't her type," Miriam Hodge said. "That doesn't mean she's homosexual."

"Don't say that word," Bea said, covering her ears. "I hate that word."

266

"Do you hate that word when someone is condemning it?" Miriam asked.

"Well, no, of course not. But that's different."

"Then it's not the word you hate. What you hate is the idea that God loves homosexuals."

This conversation was moving far beyond the Friendly Women conversational comfort zone, which was usually confined to talk of noodles and Brother Norman's shoe ministry to the Choctaw Indians. Bea Majors began gathering her things to leave. "I won't be a party to this filthy talk," she said. She tromped up the stairs, while the other Friendly Women looked on, speechless.

"Well, I hope you're proud of yourself, Miriam," Fern said. "Attacking a fellow Christian until she was forced to leave."

It had been like this ever since Deena had delivered her sermon on the mercy of God, though that wasn't what everyone was calling it. Others were referring to it as "that sermon in support of abomination, which will cause God Almighty himself to spew us out of his mouth," to quote Dale Hinshaw directly.

After a brief Christmas recess, Dale had launched an investigation that was now being dubbed Deenagate. Specifically, he's been trying to uncover how Deena rose to power on the committee so suddenly, why Sam let her preach on the biggest Sunday of the year, and, most important, the identity of the gay man she referred to in her sermon.

He'd demanded Sam's resignation immediately following the sermon, but had been fended off by Miriam Hodge and Asa Peacock. Then, as the head of the Furnace Committee, he asked for equal time in the pulpit. "If Deena gets to preach because she was head of a committee, why can't I?"

The elders thought of several reasons why, but weren't up for the fight, so they caved in and let him preach the second Sunday in January, when he clarified whom God loved and whom God didn't love. "There are certain so-called Christians," he shot a look at Sam, "who'll tell you God loves everybody, though anyone who's bothered to read the Word knows better."

The problem, as Dale saw it, began with free school lunches, which led to a welfare mentality with all sorts of people insisting on their rights, including the right to be perverted, and the government didn't do a thing about it because the liberals in Congress were running scared from the United Nations, who were trying their darndest to create a one world order, which would ultimately bring God's wrath upon Americans in general and Democrats in particular.

His sermon was an oratorical marvel, consisting of one long sentence, which Sam endured only by closing his eyes and thinking of past vacations.

Dale corralled him after church and asked him if he knew who the gay man was Deena had mentioned.

"I don't have a clue," Sam said. "And if I did, I wouldn't tell you. It's none of our business."

This was a clear dereliction of duty, as far as Dale was concerned, and the next day he wrote a letter to the Quaker superintendent in the city suggesting he replace Sam with a real minister, someone who knew the Word and didn't prattle on about God's love, which was fine in theory, but if taken seriously could lead to all sorts of depravity.

It was the third letter the superintendent had received from persons at Harmony Friends since Deena's sermon, so the last week of January, he phoned Sam and asked to meet with him.

Sam left for the city early the next day, arriving a little after nine. The superintendent kept Sam waiting outside his office for a half hour, which gave Sam time to remember why the superintendent annoyed him. He had gotten the job because his uncle was head of the search committee that hired him. The superintendent was an apostle of conformity, inclined to side with the whiners when they complained about their pastors. The last time he'd summoned Sam to his office, he'd cautioned him to stop agitating Dale, who seemed to him to be a sincere and thoughtful Christian who loved the Lord and didn't need Sam making his life more difficult. "Your job is to sell Dale on you! Show him you can deliver the goods! Can you do that, Sam?"

Before he'd become the superintendent, he'd owned a car dealership. He told anyone who'd listen that the superintendency was his way of giving back to the Lord, who'd blessed him with twenty-three years of record car sales. He talked a lot about pastors meeting their quotas and how the parishioner was always right. "If we don't make the folks in the pew happy, they'll take their tithe check and go down the street to the Methodist church. So let's go the extra mile. If you know they're goin' on vacation, offer to mow their yard and feed their pets."

Sam could barely stand to mow his own yard. Just the week before he'd proposed to Barbara that they buy a few goats to keep their grass short.

"Now what's this I hear about you promoting a homosexual agenda down there at your church?" the superintendent asked, before Sam had even settled in a chair.

"I'm doing no such thing," Sam said. "I simply invited one of our committee clerks to bring a message, and she chose to speak about that topic. I had no idea she was going to mention it."

"For crying out loud, Sam. Why'd you have to let her speak the Sunday before Christmas when everybody and their cousins are there? That's what Memorial Day Sunday's for. That's when you have someone else speak, when everyone's gone." He shook his head, baffled at Sam's ignorance.

He held up the three letters. "These people are really upset, Sam. They've asked me to investigate your theology." He shook his head in amazement. "Sam, what am I gonna do with you? Last year, I got letters that you didn't believe in God. This year, you've become a wacko liberal. What's next?"

Sam was feeling a bit peeved. "Why am I a wacko liberal just because a woman in my congregation said God loves homosexuals? What's so crazy about that?"

The superintendent eyed him up and

down. "Sam, you got to be a team player on this one. Can you do that?"

Sam looked at him warily "What do you mean?"

"I mean I don't want you to raise this subject just yet. We got to give folks time, then maybe we can talk about it. Maybe twenty years from now, when folks are ready."

Sam was trying hard to make sense of this, but it wasn't easy. He wasn't sure what to say. What would Miriam do? he wondered. "I appreciate that you don't want to upset people," he said finally. "I don't want to hurt anyone either. But are you saying we have to wait twenty years before we can say God loves gay people?"

"Now you're getting it." The superintendent smiled. "I knew you'd see it my way." He stood up from his desk. "I told my wife just this morning that you'd come around, that you were a good man, just a little ahead of your time." He walked around the desk to Sam, clapped him on the back, and ushered him toward the door. "Keep up the good work, Sam. Give Brenda my love."

"Who's Brenda?"

"Your wife."

"Her name is Barbara."

"Well, tell Barbara hello, too."

It was a long drive back home. Sam filled

the time by wondering why it was that spiritual progress was always hampered by those persons least willing to grow.

Back in Harmony, Deena was presiding over an empty Legal Grounds Coffee Shop. Ordinarily her busiest month, January had been a bust after word got out of her flirtation with enlightenment. Miriam Hodge had stopped past each day to show her support, but one person can only drink so much coffee, and Miriam was starting to bloat.

Meanwhile, Dale Hinshaw had been spending afternoons at the library reading a book on heretics. It moved Dale, learning of the various agonies visited on those who had broken God's law in the past — brandings, the removal of tongues, the guillotine. He especially admired the creativity of the Massachusetts Bay Colony, who'd lashed heretics to a great wheel and rolled them to Rhode Island. He sighed dreamily thinking of it. Those were the good old days, he thought. He photocopied the more interesting passages and mailed them to the superintendent.

He hadn't ferreted out the identity of the gay man, but was pursuing several leads. While at the library, he'd examined the due date cards on the more liberal books and discovered Ellis Hodge had signed one out the month before. That explained Miriam's tolerance for gays, Dale thought. Her own husband was one of them! He wrote down everything he knew about Ellis that supported his hunch: Ellis had refused to attend the Mighty Men of God Conference the spring before and had worn a pink shirt on Easter Sunday. (It had been white, but Miriam had inadvertently washed it with a colored load, though how was Dale to know that?)

The fact that Ellis was married didn't dampen Dale's suspicions. It was probably a clever ruse to throw people off. Dale knew for a fact Ellis had lived in the barn for an entire month the previous summer. That was probably when Miriam found him out, he speculated. That Ellis was a member of the Furnace Committee troubled Dale all the more. He'd long suspected liberal sympathizers of trying to infiltrate the one remaining God-fearing committee of Harmony Friends Meeting.

First, Ellis would seize control of the Furnace Committee, and then he'd slither his way onto the Elders Committee, where he would replace the King James pew Bibles with Bibles that called God "Mother" and "She." But it wouldn't stop there. Ellis would lobby the meeting to write a letter of support to save the redwoods or some other radical cause. There was no telling where it would end, Dale thought.

Ellis had to be stopped. That was all there was to it. It wouldn't be easy. People liked Ellis. But it had to be done. The Furnace Committee met that very week for its monthly meeting. It would have to be then. The sooner the better, so as not to let apostasy get a foothold.

They met at seven o'clock. By seven-fifteen they had fired the burners, checked the filters, and were seated at the card table.

"Who's turn is it to deal?" Asa Peacock asked.

"There won't be any card playing tonight," Dale said. "We have to have a meeting. Our faith is under attack even as we sit here."

"What's that got to do with the Furnace Committee?" Harvey Muldock asked. "We're only in charge of the furnace, and it's fine. Let's play cards."

"There's a traitor among us," Dale said. "Someone who would subvert our way of life."

Ellis chuckled. "Dale, you have to stop watching those TV ministers. They're making you crazy."

"This wasn't a TV minister. This was

Deena Morrison, right here in our own church. Talkin' about a gay man right here among us. And I know who she was talkin' about."

Harvey shifted uncomfortably in his chair. "Say Asa, I think it's my turn to deal the cards. Let's get started. I told Eunice I'd be home by ten."

Ellis eyed Dale. "I can't see the good of singling folks out like that, Dale. It's none of our business."

"Funny you of all people should feel that way," Dale said.

"What's that supposed to mean?" Ellis asked.

"I think you know what it means. Do you want to tell them or do I have to?"

"Tell them what?"

"About why you had to live in the barn last summer."

"My marriage is none of your concern, Dale Hinshaw. I'll thank you to mind your own business."

"What's the big deal about living in the barn?" Asa asked. "When we was first married, Jessie got so mad at me I had to live in the barn two whole months."

"If we're not going to play cards, I'm going home," Harvey said. "Let's get crackin'." He began dealing the cards.

Dale panicked. Ellis was getting away with it. It was time to play hardball. "Ellis, it's not too late. If you repent now, the Lord'll forgive you and you can still be on the Furnace Committee."

"What are you talking about? What am I supposed to repent about?"

"Your perversion. I know for a fact it was you Deena was talkin' about."

Ellis stared at Dale, then began to laugh. "Dale Hinshaw, you are the limit."

"You can tell us," Dale said. "It won't go any further. We'll keep it right here in the Furnace Committee. Won't we, men? Just so long as you don't go back to being a pervert."

Asa glanced up from his cards. "Hmm, that's interesting." He looked at Dale. "I figured Deena was talking about you. I always heard the folks most against gay people are usually that way themselves. But don't you worry, Dale, your secret's safe with us. We won't tell a soul, will we, guys?"

"Not a soul," Harvey agreed.

"I won't tell," Ellis added. "I figure that's between you and God and Dolores."

"If you need a barn to stay in, you can always use mine," Asa offered.

Dale was aghast.

Harvey reached across the card table and

patted Dale's hand. "It's nothing to be ashamed of. You were probably born that way. I read about it once. You probably didn't get enough testosterone when you was little."

"It doesn't change our mind about you, Dale," Ellis said. "You're still our friend, and you can still be on the Furnace Committee."

"But you need to stop talking bad about gay people," Asa said. "There's just no call for it."

"And you really should leave Deena alone," Harvey added. "She's a good kid."

Though the men could never recall Dale Hinshaw being speechless, they realized it was a difficult moment for him, so when he rose to his feet and fled the meetinghouse, they were sympathetic.

"Poor guy," Ellis said, after a bit. "Miriam and I read a book about gay people just last month. It's terrible the way people treat them. Cut off from their friends and family. Dale'll need us now more than ever."

"What I don't understand is why he keeps listening to those TV preachers," Asa said.

"Probably he thinks he can change if he just gets preached at enough about it," Harvey speculated.

Ellis shook his head at the mystery of it.

Asa studied the cards in his hand. "Right of the dealer goes first. Let's see, Harvey, I'll take two cards."

Around the table they went, betting matchsticks and lamenting Dale's predicament, until it was time for Harvey to leave and walk the three blocks home to Eunice. It was a cold night, but he was warmed by the thought that his son, Jimmy, was not alone and hopeful that, as more people like Dale faced up to who they were, compassion and understanding might one day prevail.

Nineteen
All Things Work for Good

It was a cold Saturday in February, ending one of the coldest weeks on record, which Kyle Weathers at the barbershop cited as proof that global warming was just another myth circulated by environmental wackos opposed to air-conditioning.

"Global warming, my foot," said Kyle, as he clipped the hairs from Sam's right ear. "I froze my keester walking over here this morning."

Sam didn't respond, not wanting to excite Kyle any further while he held a pointed instrument a scant inch from his eardrum.

"I tell you who started that rumor," Kyle said. "The fan companies, that's who."

"The fan companies?"

"Yes, siree. Air-conditioning gets invented and all of a sudden people don't need window fans no more, so what do the fan companies do? They start a rumor that air-conditioning causes holes in the sky, that's what they do."

"That's an interesting theory," Sam admitted.

There is a lot to learn at a barbershop, provided one can separate the wheat from the chaff. Kyle knows a great deal about hair, but is fuzzy on politics and global conspiracies, though this has not kept him from offering his opinions.

He spit on his fingers and smoothed Sam's hair flat. "You got the worst cowlicks I've ever seen."

"I've always had them," Sam said.

"Try rubbing some mayonnaise on them before you go to bed."

"I'll keep that in mind."

"So how are things going at church?" Kyle asked.

How things were going at the church was a subject Sam had hoped to avoid. Dale had been on a rampage since January when he tried to convene a heresy trial against the other members of the Furnace Committee. The rumor in the pews was that Asa, Harvey, and Ellis had put Dale in his place, though they weren't talking and Dale wasn't elaborating. The church denied Dale's request to have Asa's, Harvey's, and Ellis's tongues removed, which resulted in Dale's threatening to leave the church and take the furnace with him.

Meanwhile, the Friendly Women's Circle were laboring to finish their annual fund-raising quilt before Easter, which was coming early this year. They were making an autograph quilt. Jessie Peacock had gotten the idea from a magazine. They had mailed fabric pieces to famous people asking for autographs on them, which they were piecing together in a celebrity quilt to raffle off to the highest bidder.

It had been a contentious process. Fern Hampton was of the opinion they should confine the signatures to those luminaries who met the moral criteria of the Friendly Women. That narrowed the field considerably, and the only name they could agree upon at their first meeting was Captain Kangaroo.

"How about Jimmy Stewart?" asked Miriam Hodge. "He's a real gentleman."

"He's also dead," Opal Majors pointed out.

"I didn't know that," Miriam said. "When did that happen?"

"1997, I think it was. Remember? He was on our prayer chain."

Miriam furrowed her brow in thought. "Now that you mention it, I seem to remember something about that. Well, how about Jimmy Carter then?"

"You want someone on our quilt who told the whole world he'd lusted after women? How come we're all of a sudden so hung up on smut? First it was Deena with that sermon, now it's you, Miriam. I should think you would know better," Dolores Hinshaw said.

"Besides, he's a Democrat," Bea Majors added.

"How about Billy Graham?" asked Jessie Peacock. "He's a nice man."

"Have you seen him lately?" Dolores grumbled. "His hair is down past his collar. I don't want any beatniks on our quilt."

It took three meetings to decide on a dozen celebrities who wouldn't tarnish the Circle's wholesome reputation, though even then there were lingering doubts.

"I'm not so sure about this Nelson Mandela character," Fern Hampton had said as she stitched around his autograph. "Wasn't he a jailbird?"

A spirit of dissent had infected the entire meeting. In addition to the sporadic quarrels in the Friendly Women's Circle, Dale had asked Harvey, Asa, and Ellis to surrender their membership on the Furnace Committee.

Sam didn't volunteer this information to Kyle. Instead, he told him everything was fine and thanked him for asking. Sam wants to put forth a positive image of the church so new people will come. He's been working on Kyle for several haircuts now, extolling the virtues of the church while glossing over its defects.

He's afraid they've lost Deena. She hasn't been back since Dale had her thrown off the Peace and Social Concerns Committee the Sunday of her sermon. After his haircut, Sam stopped by the Legal Grounds Coffee Shop to visit her. It was a visit he'd been dreading; he'd put it off for two months. He hated talking with people about why they hadn't been to church. It felt like prying. They invariably complained about things he had no control over, usually something to do with Fern or Dale. The chances weren't good they were going to change.

The Legal Grounds was empty when Sam arrived, except for Deena, who was standing behind the counter. Deena smiled as he came through the door. They exchanged greetings, as he took a seat.

"So how are things at church?" she asked, as she came around and sat across from him.

He had hoped to ease into the topic, to

discuss the weather or something such as that. But Deena was her usual forthright self.

"Oh, they've settled down a bit," he said.

"I didn't realize my talking about homosexuals would cause such a stir," she said. "I'm sorry if I got you in trouble."

"Don't worry about that. It'll all work out."

"I thought maybe I should stay away until things settled down."

"It's probably as settled down as it'll ever be." He paused. "Folks sure miss you," he added.

"That's odd. No one's stopped by to visit except for Miriam."

"But you've been on everyone's mind."

Deena laughed. "I bet I have."

Their conversation wasn't turning out quite the way Sam had hoped. "Well, anyway, I just stopped by to say we missed you."

"That was kind of you, Sam. Don't worry, I'll be back. In fact, I was planning on coming to church tomorrow."

"Really?"

"Yes, I miss everyone. They kind of grow on a person."

"Yes, they do, don't they," Sam agreed.

"Besides, how can we ever change people unless we're in relationship with them?"

"Well now, there you go," Sam said. "That's a good way to look at it."

"Why don't you buy a cup of coffee, so I don't go bankrupt and have to close this place down."

"I'll do better than that. How about bringing me a chicken salad sandwich and some potato chips."

He stayed a half hour. They discussed his brother, Roger, while Sam ate. "I thought he was going to call me," Deena said. "He said he would, but he never did." She tried not to sound desperate, but she'd only had one date in nine months, and that was with a gay man.

"Roger's kind of bashful," Sam explained. "But he'll be home next month for Easter weekend. I'm sure he'd like to see you."

"Maybe we could all go out together," Deena suggested. "You and Barbara and Roger and me."

"Sure, I don't see why not. I'll ask 'em."

Sam finished his sandwich, then went back to his office to work on his sermon. He'd been planning on preaching about the prodigal son, how the son realized the error of his ways and came home, but since Deena was returning that Sunday it no longer seemed fitting. He didn't want Dale rising to his feet and pointing out the coincidence.

Instead, he wrote a sermon on how prophets were never welcome in their hometown. Let 'em chew on that, he thought, as he typed in the final sentences.

He got home just before supper. Afterward, he lit a fire in the fireplace and worked a puzzle with his sons. At nine o'clock, he and Barbara put the boys to bed, then turned on the television for the weather report. "It's warming up," Sam commented. "Only five below tonight."

"I'm faint with heat already," Barbara said.

He woke up early the next morning, ate breakfast, and arrived at the meetinghouse an hour before Sunday school. Downstairs, in the bowels of the church, the furnace was laboring away, straining to beat the cold. With the thermostat right above the heat register in Sam's office, the furnace was running constantly.

He ran through his sermon, started the coffee, and walked through the meetinghouse turning on the lights. At nine-fifteen, Miriam arrived with the doughnuts; then others began rolling in for Sunday school. They helped themselves to coffee and doughnuts, then went their separate ways — the children downstairs to the kitchen, the men to the Live Free or Die class in the meeting room up near the pulpit, the ladies to Bea Major's *Sword of the Lord* class around the folding tables in the basement, and the young adults to Sam's class on Christian discipleship in the coatroom by the door.

At ten twenty-five, Dale rang the bell signaling the end to Sunday school. They gathered in the meeting room with the Sunday school dodgers, those people who failed to see the benefit of Christian education and came just for worship. Deena was seated with the Hodges. Dale and the missus were frowning in her direction.

Bea Majors took her seat at the organ and began playing "Softly and Tenderly." She hummed along with the first two verses, then began to sing in a high, quavering voice on the third verse, "O for the wonderful love he has promised, promised for you and for me; though we have sinned he has mercy and pardon, pardon for you and for me." She glanced at Deena before launching into the chorus. "Come home, come home, ye who are weary, come home. Earnestly, tenderly, Jesus is calling — calling, 'O sinner, come home.' "

Deena looked down, studying the patterns in the carpet. Sam slumped in his chair behind the pulpit, wondering for the hundredth time what it would cost to hire a new organist.

When it appeared Bea was summoning her strength for another round, Sam rose to his feet and began praying the opening prayer even before he'd reached the pulpit. He skipped the joys and concerns part of worship. He didn't want anyone standing and saying what a joy it was to see Deena back in church, putting her on the spot. He had them sing an extra song instead. Then he began his sermon.

He spoke about the temptation to reject persons who bring news we don't want to hear but need to hear. People didn't seem to understand he was talking about Deena. They were yawning and glancing at their watches. He thought of mentioning Deena by name. That would get their attention. But decided against it for fear of embarrassing her.

He finished his sermon, then settled into silence. Five minutes passed. Sam heard a slight pinging noise. He looked up and glanced around. There was more pinging, then a screeching noise of metal against metal. Smoke began to pour out the heat registers.

There were a few cries of alarm. The men of the Furnace Committee glanced at one another. Fortunately, they had prepared for just such an emergency. Ellis, Asa, Harvey, and Dale began evacuating the meetinghouse, women and children first. Sam was the last to leave, the captain of the ship taking the last lifeboat to safety.

They stood clutched in a knot out on the sidewalk in the bitter cold. Off in the distance, they could hear the wail of the fire alarm, summoning the volunteer firefighters to the station.

Suddenly, a scream pierced the air. "Our autograph quilt!" Fern Hampton shrieked. "It's still in the basement! I'm going in!" She lumbered toward the meetinghouse door.

"No, Fern," Deena said. "You stay here. I'll get it." And before anyone could stop her, she rushed into the meetinghouse. She opened the front door and smoke billowed out. She dropped to her knees and crawled inside.

"Oh, Lord, she's going to be burnt to a turn," Jessie Peacock moaned.

Minutes ticked by like hours.

"I'm going after her," Asa Peacock said, putting a handkerchief from his pocket to cover his mouth.

"I never should have said anything," Fern wailed. "She's dead in there. I just know it."

Deena came out just as Asa neared the

front door. The quilt was gathered in her arms. She was bent over coughing as Asa guided her down the steps.

"Oh, thank you, Lord. She's safe," Fern said, weeping. She drew Deena to her and began pounding her back, causing Deena to expel puffs of smoke.

The wail of a siren split the air as the fire truck careened around the corner and pulled up in front of the meetinghouse. "Everybody get back," Darrell Furbay, the fire chief, yelled. "Get in your cars, so's you don't freeze."

The firemen began unrolling their hoses, while Darrell pulled on his oxygen mask and ambled into the meetinghouse. He emerged several minutes later and ordered the men to roll up the hoses. "Furnace motor," he said. "You get a furnace motor burning out and it looks a lot worse than it is, on account of the smoke goes through the heat registers. Don't look like it's that old of a furnace to me. Probably still under warranty. I'd call the fella that put it in if I were you. Looks awful small for the size of the church. I think the motor overheated trying to heat all this space. Whoever put it in shoulda put a bigger one in. Anyway, I got it shut off for now, but you'll want to get it replaced quick so your water pipes don't freeze and bust."

Dale called an emergency meeting of the Furnace Committee at his house. They phoned his son, Robert Dale, who was singularly unhelpful. There wasn't a warranty, he explained. He'd purchased the furnace from a friend's cousin in the city who'd bought it at an auction.

It was all Asa, Harvey, and Ellis could do to hold their tongues. They had suspected all along that hiring Robert Dale to install the furnace would result in this.

Dale said, "Well, looks like we're going to need a new furnace. I think we oughta hire Robert Dale to put it in."

"You gotta be kidding," Harvey said. "We wouldn't even have been in this mess if he knew what he was doing in the first place."

"Well, he knows better now, and I think we oughta forgive and forget, just like the Word teaches."

They haggled back and forth before agreeing to give Robert Dale the chance to redeem himself. "But no more threatening to kick us off the committee," Ellis said to Dale. "And from now on, you don't have any more say than we do."

"It's a deal," Dale said grudgingly, clearly unhappy.

As for the ladies of the Circle, Deena offered the use of the Legal Grounds so they could finish their quilt. "We don't deserve your kindness," Fern said. "We've not been very nice to you."

"Don't think a thing of it," Deena said. "I'm grateful for the company. I've been kind of lonely lately."

"We're gonna find you a man if it takes the rest of our lives," Bea vowed.

They set up the quilting frame in the Legal Grounds that afternoon and draped the quilt across it to air out. It reeked of smoke. When Deena opened the next morning the odor had permeated the shop. This won't do, she thought. She gathered up the quilt and carried it to the washing machine in the back room. She turned the knob to "gentle" and set it for an extra rinse cycle. After the washer stopped, she lifted it out and moved it to the dryer. Forty-five minutes later the buzzer sounded. She pulled the quilt out, rolled it onto the frame, and was horrified to see twelve empty squares, devoid of signatures, staring back.

She studied the quilt closely, trying to make out the signatures. Not a trace remained. She felt sick to her stomach, on the verge of nausea. Why hadn't they used permanent markers? she wondered. How would she ever tell the Friendly Women what she had done? They were coming that morning to finish the quilt. Maybe they won't notice, she thought. No, there was no chance of that. It was too obvious. And just when she was getting back in their good graces.

The Friendly Women arrived within the hour. Deena was still trying to figure out how to tell them when Dolores Hinshaw noticed the autographs were gone.

"I knew this would happen," she wailed. "The Lord sent an angel to erase the names. When he couldn't destroy the quilt in a fire, he found another way. I knew this would happen. I was against this quilt from the start. Didn't he tell us in the book of James to make no distinction between the rich and the poor? And here we are making a celebrity quilt. We're lucky he didn't smite the whole lot of us."

Fern bent down and sniffed the quilt. "This quilt has been washed. I can smell the detergent. Someone washed this."

They stared at one another.

"It was me," Deena confessed, on the edge of tears. "It reeked of smoke, so I washed it. I thought the names were in permanent marker."

The women stared at her, dismayed.

"I'm sorry," she said. "I'll pay you whatever you think it's worth."

The women studied the quilt. A few

began to weep. "Maybe Dolores was right," Bea said, after a few minutes. "Maybe this was the Lord's way of sending us a message."

"I never was for this quilt," said Fern. "I just went along with it because I thought everyone else wanted it. I think you'll recall that I suggested we make a Scripture quilt."

"It's not too late," Miriam pointed out. "We could stitch twelve Bible verses on it in no time."

"That's a fine idea," Jessie said.

"Just so long as there's nothing from the Song of Solomon," Bea added. "We've had enough talk about sex lately."

It took them several meetings to pick out twelve verses they could agree on. The women wanted the verses to be upbeat, but Dolores Hinshaw insisted on a passage from Revelation about the lake of fire.

It took them the rest of February to stitch the Bible verses. By then, the meetinghouse furnace was replaced, but the Circle elected to remain in the Legal Grounds after Deena offered a 10 percent discount on coffee and sandwiches. Even with the discount, she was back in the black in two weeks' time.

Sam stopped past every morning on his way to the meetinghouse, visiting with the ladies as they finished the quilt. They were pleased with his interest, though curious about why he now smelled like mayonnaise.

As for Sam, he was glad the autograph quilt had gone by the wayside. It had troubled his egalitarian spirit, though he hadn't said anything for fear of offending the Circle. It warmed his heart to see Deena and the Friendly Women reconciled, stitching a Scripture quilt to the glory of God.

It was a radiant quilt, the colors tastefully coordinated, the lettering attractive and precise. Dolores's verse on the lake of fire was tucked in the corner, scarcely visible, where all bad theology belongs. Romans 8:28 occupied the center patch — *We know that in everything God works for good with those who love him, who are called according to his purpose.*

It was as fine a way to enter Lent as a church could hope for. Deena Morrison in the good graces of the Circle, Dale unseated from his throne on the Furnace Committee, a glorious Scripture quilt to hang behind the pulpit on Easter Sunday, and a brand-new furnace to boot.

It was, Sam Gardner thought, enough to make the most callous soul believe in a benevolent God. And though he worried about Dale and prayed for him to soften, he resolved to be patient.

"In your time, in your way," he prayed to the Lord. "But please forgive me if I should plead with you to hurry it up."

In addition to writing, Philip Gulley also enjoys the ministry of speaking. If you would like more information, please contact:

David Leonards
3612 North Washington Boulevard
Indianapolis, IN 46205-3592
317-926-7566
ieb@prodigy.net

About the Author

Philip Gulley is a Quaker minister, writer, husband, and father. He is the bestselling author of *Front Porch Tales*, *Home to Harmony*, *Just Shy of Harmony*, and *Christmas in Harmony*.

He and his wife, Joan, live in Indiana with their sons, Spencer and Sam.

The employees of Thorndike Press hope you have enjoyed this Large Print book. All our Thorndike and Wheeler Large Print titles are designed for easy reading, and all our books are made to last. Other Thorndike Press Large Print books are available at your library, through selected bookstores, or directly from us.

For information about titles, please call:

(800) 223-1244

or visit our Web site at:

www.gale.com/thorndike
www.gale.com/wheeler

To share your comments, please write:

Publisher
Thorndike Press
295 Kennedy Memorial Drive
Waterville, ME 04901